I0663840

Steven Milner and the Slightly Legendary Band

written by
Andrew Milner

Visit my website at *https://linktr.ee/AndrewMilner*
Find me on Instagram: @andrewmilnermusic

Table of Contents

Prologue

The land of Canterevia's history is synonymous with music. In the world where this land exists, everything related to how you and I perceive music can be traced back to this location, from the first violin and guitar-like instruments, to people singing in the center market place about daily events.

In time, each instrument evolved, until eventually they reached the forms we all know and use today in our world. They say that people became so good at making music, that word spread to neighboring lands, who all began long and arduous journeys in the hopes that they get to experience the beauty of Canterevia's music.

As time went on, though, not all visitors had the best of intentions. In fact, in what would be the 18th century in our timeline, some if these visitors stopped hiding their intent.

The Canterevians had heard of invading forces from far away lands. And while the names given to them were many, researchers can safely conclude that they were committing acts of conquest and spoke a similar tongue to what people today know as English.

As such, in their research, they simply refer to them as English people. All of this does explain how in the present day you have a mix of English and Latin-based names and naming conventions in Canterevia.

You would think that based on this, the English easily won the battle, but fate had other ideas. As the battle was about to begin, a third force, which researchers concluded would have been classified as being of Spanish origins in our world, attempted to seize the land of music.

As such, the Canterevians and the English made a pact and managed to defeat this 3rd force together, forging an alliance that is still ongoing to this day. The English people learned all about how to make music, and the Canterevians benefitted from this world's equivalent of the industrial revolution, transforming the land and allowing those who wanted to explore other areas of work to have the opportunity to do so.

And while people still give you weird looks when you say you're from Canterevia and want to do something other than music, it is very much accepted that different career paths exist there today.

The leaders of Canterevia didn't want to risk the land losing its music-centered identity though, so they made sure to have a city dedicated to allowing and creating the best musicians in their world.

Some people suggested that that city be the capital, Cantasia, but in the end, a city near the capital was chosen to become the land's music hub. That city's name is Monodia, and it's located approximately 50 kilometers from the capital city.

It's quite a beautiful city, separated into six districts, and traversed by the river Rotondo. It retains a lot of the Roman-like architecture that Canterevia is famous for, while also having acres of green spaces, woods, and a beautiful hills district, where they say adults go and contemplate life decisions while driving to whatever soundtrack they desire.

And it is here in this city where our stories take place. Now, in Canterevia, the years are numbered differently, but we can assume based on findings, that the story we're about to hear starts in what would be the year 2025 in the outer world (the one you and I live in).

This outer world is not accessible to those who live in Canterevia, but there are some people who claim they can reference events and people from it. No one really believes them though, with the most common saying being that they are glitching from too much creativity in their minds.

Whether or not this is true is up for debate, so each and every reader of these tales should decide for themselves. So, without further ado, let us begin...

First day of high school

"Please move slower, it's everyone's dream to start high school with a reprimand for being late...", a rather anxious Adrian Milner said while humming the tune to a song about a safari, or love, or both.

The first day of high school was about to start for twin brothers Steven and Adrian Milner, and one could say that at least one of them was a bit nervous.

Adrian was all dressed up and ready to go. It was not hard to understand why, since his usual attire consisted of jeans and a grey t-shirt.

And given that he had short hair, it was even easier to save time in getting ready. Steven, on the other hand...

"I don't think they give you reprimands for being late on the first day. Nevertheless, we have about...two minutes and 37 seconds to go, according to your schedule", replied Steven while delicately combing his long hair, all the while making sure his shirt would not get wrinkled.

"Wait, how do you know about that? I never told you anything", asked Adrian.

"You were mumbling it in your sleep."

"So now you're watching me while I'm sleeping?" a slightly bewildered Adrian asked.

"No, as it turns out, I am forced to listen to you while you are sleeping. On the other hand, I am done, and we should be ready to go."

Adrian breathed a sigh of relief and they both went to put their shoes on and grabbed their backpacks.

"Aww, look at you both, all dressed up and ready to go", the boys' mother said with an emotional voice.

They both awkwardly smiled, not knowing exactly how to react.

"Quick, before you go, let's take a photo. And Adrian, can you do your mother a favor and smile for a bit? And I am talking about a real smile, not a robotic one."

Adrian was not really in the mood, but managed to look happy in the photo, or so he hoped.

"Let's see...yeah, all good, such a lovely photo", their mother said joyfully. She then continued:

"Now then, off you go. Steven, darling, don't forget your sunglasses. And Adrian, don't forget to take good care of your noise cancelling headphones."

"Yes, Mom", said the two in unison.

With everything ready, Adrian and Steven went outside, where their father was waiting to drive them to school.

The ride proved to be quite smooth and in just under 10 minutes, they arrived at Andrew F. Gordon High School, located in the Sonata Gardens district, which was the same district that the boys lived in.

The school ground was bustling with energy, anxiety, joy, and many other emotions as a new group of students was getting ready to start their high school adventures.

After they arrived, Steven and Adrian hugged their father and went inside the courtyard. Adrian looked around, taking it all in, and observing the students around him.

He noticed a few people from his elementary school, including someone who, at some point, he'd hoped would have gone to another high school.

Noticing this, Steven asked:

"So, is your crush on that Monica girl over or not?"

"I don't know, honestly. I'm just hoping that our classrooms are not on the same floor", answered Adrian.

The boys looked around, trying to figure out where their classmates were.

At this point, we should take a moment to understand how the school system in this world functions.

Children usually attend kindergarten from ages 5 to 7, followed by elementary school, which is divided into two parts. The first part, grades 1 to 4, features a single teacher for all subjects.

The second phase covers grades 5 to 8, with each class led by a different professor to help students adjust to high school life.

After elementary school, students take exams on grades 5 to 8 material, and the scores determine their eligibility for their chosen high school.

As such, high school usually starts for children at age 15 and lasts four years, after which students can either go to a university or enter the working field.

Steven and Adrian had high enough scores for Michael Bryan Sanders High School, the best in town, but chose not to attend mainly due to its long distance from home.

Sanders High, located in the city center district, which is also known as the Passaggio District, was about a 45-minute journey, while the one they had chosen instead, Andrew F. Gordon High School, was a few bus stops away and even in walking distance if the weather allowed it.

Each year, four new classes of around 20 students are created in each high school, with adjustments made if needed. Students can choose from classes focused on mathematics and computer programming, mathematics and literature, arts, philosophy, and history, or a general class covering various subjects.

While Steven and Adrian were tempted by the arts class, their parents insisted on them going to the mathematics and literature one, which they did end up being a part of.

As they were wandering around in the courtyard, Steven tried to calm his brother's nervousness, by asking him about his guitar:

"You know, when you were building your guitar with Dad last year, I was surprised you didn't go for gold striped on that red wood color."

"Such a transformation needs to be earned, so I decided to go with something a bit more neutral, like this bright blue. Also, when me and Dad worked on creating this guitar, I didn't feel any back-tingling so gold wasn't really an option."

"Well, you could start with juice, push-ups and sit-ups...you know, to keep up with your outside world references."

"Eh, maybe one day I'll-"

The boys were rudely interrupted by a nosy girl commenting on their appearance:

"Aww, look at these two, all dressed up and ready to be the unpopular kids in the next 4 years."

Taken aback by these comments, Steven was a bit confused. Adrian on the other hand was completely calm and started analyzing the person talking to them.

"What's the matter, is this the first time a girl other than your mother has talked to you?"

Adrian's left eyebrow flinched for a bit. He still wasn't saying anything, but was trying to figure out as much as he could about this girl. He noticed a very worn bracelet on her left hand.

Snapping out of his confusion, Steven said:

"Listen...uhm...I didn't quite catch your name there."

"Nice move, I bet a lot of guys would love to think that fast..."

Adrian then whispered something to Steven, and the obnoxious girl saw it:

"Did he tell you he's about to cry?"

"No, he just told me to call you girl-dressed-as-a-pop-punk-third-rate-act since you're obnoxious, loud, and should have guitars masking your voice because it's grating to the ears."

Now it was the girl's turn to be taken aback.

"Who in the...what is that even supposed to mean?" she asked in a very confused tone.

"It means your vocal recording track would get auto-muted in digital audio workstations when playing back the whole song. Also, you dress like you travelled to the outer world and are failing to rock the look of a woman destined to marry a guy that keeps telling people to look at a photograph because every time he does it, it makes him laugh for some reason. Now, what was that you were saying about our mother?" said Adrian in a terrifyingly firm voice.

The girl was now the one without a comeback line.

"Sheesh, I just said she made you dress up really good for the first day of high school. What, did I hit a nerve or something?" she asked, trying to keep her cool.

Steven then realized where this was going...

"Look, girl-whose-name-we-don't-yet-know, I highly, highly suggest you drop this now. Trust me, it's in everyone's best interest if you do so", he said, also trying to keep a calm voice.

"What's he going to do otherwise, go into more rants about guitar volumes, muting, or fashion?" the girl asked.

"No, I'm going to hit one of your nerves", Adrian responded calmly.

"Oh, really? What's mommy's boy going to do?" asked the girl with a mocking voice.

Adrian leaned towards her so only she could hear him and said in a soft voice:

"Your outburst tells me you've worked really hard at concealing whatever traumatic event you're wearing on your left-hand wrist. If you turn around and walk away, we forget any of this ever happened, you confirm I am right, and you get to keep your dignity and sanity. But should you choose to dispute this...well, I think we both know we don't want that scene happening now, do we? Oh, and before you leave, is this good enough of a nerve-touching moment from this momma's boy or not?"

The girl was now really scared, sad, and a bit angry. However, she chose to walk away instead of saying anything else.

"What did you say to her?" asked Steven after she was out of sight.

"Nothing and everything at the same time. She has unresolved issues, I don't know or care exactly what they are. But at least she's out of here and I'm thinking she won't be bothering us too much. She should have listened to you", replied Adrian.

"Aren't you worried she'll do something bad now?" a worried Steven asked.

"Given that I didn't shout it for the whole world to hear, no. As it stands, I don't know anything concrete, she knows I know something bad happened, but that's it."

"Still, whatever happened was pretty bad. She had a great deal of sadness in her eyes when you told her off."

Adrian noticed a bit of longing on Steven's face, which even his sunglasses couldn't fully hide. He thought to himself: *"For someone like me who prides himself on not being easily shaken, this is truly testing those limits..."*

While still a bit annoyed by this interaction, the boys finally found their classmates and went to their classroom.

All of them were greeted by Audrey Stevens, their homeroom teacher. Each class had a teacher responsible for overseeing that specific classroom, fostering a certain class culture and structure, and gathering feedback about the students from other teachers.

"Good morning, dear students", professor Stevens said. "Now, let's get seated, please."

Steven and Adrian were in a class with 16 other students, and they were going to sit at desks arranged for pairs. Their classroom featured three rows, each containing three separate desks. The twins chose to sit at the middle desk in the middle row.

"Now everyone, my name is Audrey Stevens and I am both your homeroom and mathematics teacher. On your desks, you will find your daily schedule, as well as the names of the teachers for each course you will be attending in your freshman year."

Everyone in class took a few moments to check out their schedules to see what they should expect. To their relief, it seemed that Friday was quite the easy day, with no math classes in sight.

"Did everyone get a chance to go through their schedules?" professor Stevens asked.

"Yes, professor", a slightly detuned choir of voices answered.

"*Good thing I have these headphones on*", Adrian thought to himself.

"Excellent. I think now is a good time to get to know one-another. Let's start with...the boy with headphones, which I am going to assume are not being currently used to listen to music", professor Stevens said looking towards Adrian.

"No, professor, they are not", said Adrian, standing up. "They are actually noise cancelling headphones that help reduce the ambient noise that would otherwise impair my hearing quite a lot."

"Would you be so kind as to elaborate a bit?" asked professor Stevens.

"Not a problem. Basically, I have something called perfect pitch, which means I can instantly identify the pitch of any given sound. And supposedly I can also produce any pitch at will", answered Adrian.

"That's actually interesting, but why do you require headphones?"

"Because if I am exposed to too much noise for prolonged periods of time, it might actually pose a threat to my hearing and well-being, not to mention my ability to focus. I worked with a hearing-aid specialist to develop them so as to not impair my ability to listen to whoever is speaking to me though. It seems to be some form of misophonia, but not the usual one, since it occurs...basically when it wants to."

"I understand. And your name is..."

"Adrian Milner is my name, professor."

"Excellent. Thank you for your presentation, Adrian. Now, let's move on to your desk mate."

Adrian's desk mate was gazing into the distance, some three different dimensions and voids away.

"Psst, as Adrian's desk mate, it's your turn", whispered Adrian towards Steven.

"My turn to what?" asked Steven as though he just woke up.

Everybody in the classroom chuckled, including professor Stevens.

"To tell us a bit about yourself", said the professor.

"Oh, that...right. My name's Steven Milner and despite valiant efforts from this lovable hunk of walking sarcasm here to prove the contrary, I can confirm we are in fact twins", replied Steven.

Everybody in the classroom chuckled once again. Even Adrian showed signs of an amused smirk.

"Also, if you ever need an Adrian-to-English translator, I can most likely help you with that."

"I can't help but notice that, unlike other sets of twins around this planet, you chose to have two wildly different looks", a curious professor Stevens remarked.

"That is actually a funny story. We both would have wanted to have long hair, but he lost a coin flip and a best-out-of-three console football game challenge, so he had to concede this time around. In time, Adrian also realized it would have been way too hard to maintain it and he became really happy with the outcome. Not sure about the match results though..."

"Interesting. Thank you very much for the information, Steven. Now, let's move on to the other students as well."

With their introduction out of the way, Adrian and Steven both got to relax and try to learn a bit about their classmates.

Turns out there were 9 guys and 9 girls in their classroom and all of them seemed pretty tame in terms of personalities, at least for now.

Adrian was also on the lookout for potential band members, because he wanted to form a band to take part in the local high school Battle of the Bands, which took place year after year between the four high schools in their local town.

To his great delight, he noticed some potential members in the form of three other boys who voiced a strong interest in music. Adrian made sure to remember their names.

Callum was a boy with brown curly hair who said he was a fan of heavy metal music and wanted to learn to play the guitar. Jack, another boy with black hair, studied classical guitar and was open to playing the bass guitar. Lastly, there was Parker, a boy with straight black hair and glasses, who was studying the drums.

"*Hm, no one interested in being a lead singer...that may pose a problem*", Adrian thought to himself.

The rest of the day went on without any noticeable events and soon, the boys were on their way home.

Steven then remembered the early day encounter:

"You know, I was thinking about the girl from earlier..."

"What about her?"

"I don't know...something felt off, like she was trying to be someone she's not. What's your take?"

"She was lashing out due to something bad that happened, but I don't really want to waste my time thinking about it too much", said Adrian.

"Well, I always like to think there's good inside each and every person, her included. I just...don't exactly know what to do when we run into her again."

"When? There's like 300 or so students in this high school, we can blend in and avoid her with ease."

"So, I take it you don't believe that much in giving her a second chance should the occasion show itself?" a somewhat disheartened Steven asked.

"I believe in second chances but I just don't see the need to offer it to people who go out of their way to behave like that towards other people they don't know."

"Maybe she was having a bad day", said Steven as the two of them left the courtyard.

"Do you see me lashing out at people when I'm having a bad day?" asked Adrian in an assertive tone.

"Only at digital versions of real-life football players", answered Steven with an amused smirk.

"Precisely my point."

As the two boys continued their walk home, Adrian couldn't help but think about what his brother was suggesting. He knew they'd run into that girl again and he feared awkward encounters more than he let on.

Adrian was certain of very few things, but two of them were in a bit of a contradiction here. He knew that when Steven felt good vibes coming from a person, he was almost always right. And he knew that he was almost always right in never giving second chances to people who behaved like that girl.

"Is this some sort of sick joke that fate is playing on me with this girl? Is Steven right about her? Or am I right about her? What on Earth am I supposed to do when

we do run into her again? Hm, I definitely need a distraction from this...", Adrian thought to himself.

"Hey, Steven, want to take a small detour to the comic-book shop before we go home?"

"Yeah, that sounds like a good idea. Let's go!"

Comic book mishaps

The city of Monodia is located some 60 kilometers south of Cantasia, the capital city of Canterevia. In the northern part of Monodia is the district called Rondo Heights, famous for its scenic roads, views, and the highway that leads into Cantasia.

After passing the river Rotondo via the main bridge, you enter the city center district, which is known as the Passaggio District, since it offers a direct passage to all the other districts.

The eastern district is called Allievo Grove, while the western one is Cantore West Side, which is located very close to the river Rotondo. Sonata Gardens is the southern district, where the Milners currently reside, and it is located right next to The Abandoned Quarters, a district that is in the process of a rebuild, with the only building yet to be torn down being that of a former office building.

Monodia is a medieval style city, with legends saying there once used to be a castle somewhere near the Rondo Heights area. In time, it has welcomed more modern buildings as well, especially in the city center, but they manage to blend in quite nicely.

As Steven and Adrian were walking down the sidewalk and enjoying what turned out to be a lovely Monday afternoon, they soon arrived at The Multiverse Junction, the local comic book store, located somewhere in the middle of the Sonata Gardens area.

This store recently celebrated its 50-year anniversary and was one of the most popular places for teenagers from all areas of the town. Featuring a wide array of comic books and manga from all genres, some even based on local musicians' careers, it was a sure place to find something good to read for just about anyone.

Adrian opened the door and the twins were welcomed by the sound of the lovely shop chime, telling the cashier that someone new has entered, and the unmistakable smell of a book store, with just a hint of freshly squeezed orange juice and pastry.

Inside, there were quite a few people going about, trying to find something good to read. Adrian was glad that he could finally take his headphones off, as it was sufficiently quiet for him not to be affected in any way.

The store itself was large enough to accommodate both comics, manga, and a bar area where people could buy drinks and certain types of pastry and other treats for when they wanted to unwind. You were allowed to read comics there as well, with the mention that should you damage the comic books or manga in any way, you would be obligated to buy them.

"Ah, if it isn't Adrian and long-haired Adrian", said the person behind the cashier desk.

"Yeah, figured we'd drop by for a quick reading session", responded Adrian. "How goes business today?"

"Quite well, even if it is the first day of school and most teens are busy", said Dennis, as he was checking out something on his laptop.

"Cool. We'll take a look around and be right back", said Adrian.

Dennis is an old friend of Adrian and Steven and is a year older than them. He started working part-time at the comic book store in order to help his family out, as they were a bit strapped for cash.

Adrian then started looking over some manga which was still entertaining to him, even though he read it about five times already. Steven joined him shortly.

After a while, they heard a somewhat familiar voice, which was anything but pleased:

"Dennis, where is that latest purchase report? We seem to be missing two packs of still water for the bar."

"It's right here sir. You told me to order 12 packs and I ordered 12 packs."

"No, you didn't. Only 10 arrived", the annoyed voice added.

"Ok, I'll take a look at it and-"

"Well, you better do that and better hope you did in fact order all 12 because otherwise, you're in big trouble."

Noticing this, Adrian swiftly came up with a plan:

"Listen, go ask that rather annoyed boss type person for help about something. I don't really care what, just get him away from Dennis for about five minutes", he said to Steven.

Steven was giddy, as he rarely gets to help out Adrian do some mischievous stuff. So, with a giant smile on his face, he went towards Dennis' boss.

He quickly went to a more neutral face as he got closer and said the following:

"Sir, sorry to interrupt, but I think I heard some movement next to the food at the bar. It might be a stray cat or a rat."

"What? Oh, bloody Hell...", the annoyed boss said as he went to check out what was going on. Steven followed him, giving two thumbs up and a giant smile to Adrian and Dennis. He wanted to try and keep the boss busy if he should find nothing, which was in fact what he was going to find if left unchecked.

Adrian swooped in next to Dennis:

"We got about five minutes, tell me what's wrong, what needs to be fixed, and how oblivious angry-boss-man over there is when it comes to technology."

"Right, so I did mess up and two packs are missing. I can work on ordering them right now but I need a passable solution as to why I only ordered 10. And he's completely oblivious to anything computer-related."

"Got it. How do you usually order stuff for the bar?"

"This form right here", said Dennis showing Adrian the ordering form.

Adrian quickly analyzed the form and saw what fields were required. He saw that the field for quantity was free text, which gave him an idea.

"What's your website built in? Is it using a content management system type thing or a custom solution?"

"Yeah, like he'd ever shell out money for a custom solution", chuckled Dennis.

Adrian was no software development expert, but he did manage to pick up a few things while watching his father build websites for clients a few years back:

"I need the admin login, quick."

Dennis then logged into the admin section of the website and Adrian quickly searched for the ordering form page, found it, and set a default value to the quantity field.

He noticed that the boss was closing in, but luckily, Steven found a way to delay him a bit, by "accidentally" spilling a glass of water.

"Right, default value is set to 10, you now remember that you entered 12, but encountered an error and the damn computer reset the value to 10 when you ordered", whispered Adrian in one breath as the boss was coming back.

"So, got any explanations Dennis?"

"Uhm, yes, sir. So, see here, when we order these packs sir, we enter the amount here. Now, when I last created an order, this computer gave me an error and set the value to 10. I have called the providers and two packs are now on their way."

The boss was a bit suspicious of this explanation, as it seemed to tie everything together way too easy for his liking.

"Show me the page as if you were creating a new order", he said.

Hoping everything would work out, Dennis refreshed the page and to his and Adrian's great delight, the default value worked and it was showing 10.

"Blasted computers. This is why everything worked better before, good old pen and paper and none of these bloody default somethings to ruin everything", muttered the boss.

He was getting ready to leave for his office but noticed Adrian standing there:

"And what is it you want, young man?"

"I'm just...waiting to ask Dennis here about some comics."

"Very well. The last thing I need is some other teenagers sending me on wild cats and rats chases", the boss muttered, giving an innocent looking Steven a somewhat angry stare, before going into his office.

"That was way too close for comfort", a relieved Dennis said as he removed the default value. "Thank you ever so much, you quite literally saved my job right there."

"Don't mention it. It was quite fun. Plus, without you around here, who else is going to let us hang around here unbothered?", said Adrian.

"Fair enough. I do want to repay you two though for your help, as I can't afford to lose this job. Is there anything you want to get, on the house?" a grateful Dennis said.

"Dennis, we both know your situation and the last thing we want is for you to get into trouble and possibly lose money", said Steven, and Adrian nodded in agreement.

"You're too kind, but can't I interest you in anything? I wouldn't offer it if I knew I couldn't do it."

The boys then thought for a bit. After a few seconds, Steven came up with a proposal:

"So, we managed to get into it with someone on our first day and I'm fairly sure I heard some mean comments from another jock-type class mate. A place to lay low and chill would do wonders, especially for special-ears over here. Do you think you can have a table reserved for us at all times should we need it? You know, like helping us make this our band headquarters while we're in high school? That is of course if you can get it past angry-boss-man."

"You're in a band?" asked Dennis.

"Well, there is an idea of a band. We're uhm...still working out some details, I guess?"

"I see. Angry-boss-man is oblivious to most things that need to be done on any form of technology. Plus, the bar area is quite large, so I think I can manage it quite easily", said Dennis.

"Awesome! Do you think that table to the far-right corner could work? It's not as visible as the rest and I assume it's not that sought out for, given how I don't think I've ever seen it occupied."

"Yeah, that's the one I had in mind as well", added Adrian. "It would also provide some good thinking space because of the silence and all. Mind if I check it out a bit?"

"Yeah, go ahead", said Dennis.

Steven stayed behind and when Adrian was far enough away, he asked Dennis:

"Listen, if it's not a big enough hassle, do you think I can store some supplies for...emergencies?"

"Emergencies?"

"Yeah, like if I need a backup pair of headphones or some Rubik's cubes for Adrian."

"Oh yeah, I have just the place for that here and only I have access to it. I know you said emergencies, but so long as you somehow manage to time them during my working hours here, I'll gladly help you."

"Excellent. Here they are. Please, take good care of them", said Steven giving him a pair of headphones and three Rubik's cubes.

Dennis put the supplies in his storage space just as Adrian was returning. It's important to note that one of Adrian's ways to figure out solutions to just about any problem, big or small, was to fiddle around with a Rubik's cube.

"Yeah, that table's perfect. So, you're sure it's no problem?"

"Yes Adrian, all is good."

"Awesome. Thank you very much Dennis."

"No worries."

The twins then looked around for a bit more and they decided to get a special edition with a variant cover of one of their favorite comic books. After that, they started their walk home.

"Well, that was quite a productive first day of school", remarked Steven.

"I guess we could call it that, though I was hoping for no annoying interactions. It doesn't put me in the right frame of mind, but at least I was able to see some potential band members. I suppose we should try and talk to them about it in the following days", said Adrian.

"You still seem a little distraught."

"I'm fine, just a bit tired."

Adrian was lying. He was in fact still a bit distraught by the events of the day, but he at least managed to get his overthinking under control for now.

Monodia Battle of the Bands

Established in its current form sometime in the 19th century, Monodia made a name for itself as the place where the greatest musicians in the world are born. And in the year of our outside world timeline 1950, the city council decided they wanted to symbolize their role in music history by creating an annual event based around music.

There were many ideas, such as a yearly festival headlined by artists who have made a career and were either born in Monodia or have studied there. Some others have said than an annual workshop about songwriting would work the best.

However, the idea that had the most success was one put together by the headmasters of the four public high schools in the city, which, by the way, were named after the four musicians who played a pivotal role in forging the allegiance between Canterevia and the English forces.

These high schools are Andrew F. Gordon High School, located in the Sonata Gardens district, Michael Bryan Sanders High School, located in the city center area, Brooks R. Hawkins High School, located in Allievo Grove, and Richard B. Maddison Riverside High School, located in Cantore West Side.

The general idea was to have their best musically-inclined students compete in a yearly battle of the bands style competition. At first, the competition started with the bands playing only covers from other artists, national and international.

The rules were simple at first. When students started high school, there would be a competition draw where each high school would be assigned two bands which they would need to play covers from.

Then, throughout the ninth and tenth grades, each high school would allow their students to practice for the elimination round at the end of the tenth grade, where each high school would hold a shoot-out between the four best bands, as chosen by other student listeners. The winner based on the judge's votes would end up competing in the actual competition, which would take place the following year just before summer break.

The headmasters argued that this would allow all students to be fully focused on their final year of high school and college admissions without any other outside interruption.

Throughout the years, the rules regarding the songs that bands played varied from covers to a combination of covers and originals. To provide variety, each and every year, the musical genres would change, and for this edition, the focus would be on rock and metal genres and subgenres.

Adrian and Steven were fully convinced that for their competition cycle, they would be playing only covers. However, as their second day of high school began, they received their official rulebook for this competition cycle and were left a bit stunned, to say the least:

"Original songs based on rock and metal genres?" asked their entire classroom in unison.

"*Huh, now there's a twist...*", Adrian thought to himself.

"Yes, you read that correctly", professor Stevens said. "The competition organizers thought a bit of a shake-up was required in order to encourage students to become better songwriters as well."

"But I was under the impression that our headmaster was in favor of the covers-only approach", a slightly anxious Callum noted.

"Yes, but he was overruled in votes, three to one. And given that our high school hasn't really had any notable performances in the last...almost two decades now, it's not really a surprise. You can't really have any sort of influence when you're the punchline for every joke your competition makes", added professor Stevens.

She then started gazing into the distance, with a look of sadness on her face.

"I am an alumnus of this high school. I never got into a band or much into music. When your generation has to participate, it could possibly be 21 years without us winning as a school. I'd very much wish for that drought to end with a band that forms in this classroom..."

After another brief pause, professor Stevens continued:

"The presentation event at Sanders High is tomorrow. You'll learn further details there, but for starters, the main genres for your competition are heavy metal and punk, and the rules specify that there should be between 10 and 20 songs. This will be quite a challenging task!"

She then added:

"Additionally, the presentation requires an actual student or band from each high school to be there, though having a full band might give us a better look and less snarky comments. There haven't been any volunteers from other classes, so I'm asking here: Is anyone interested in participating? Like I said, it will take place tomorrow at Michael Bryan Sanders High School."

"Of course, the high school with the most wins gets this honor as well. Like they need the attention and

publicity...", Adrian thought to himself before raising his hand and saying:

"Professor, me and Steven would like to go. And if you say that having a band gives a better look, we could also take three other classmates with us as well."

"Are you sure you weren't talked into the last part by those three classmates?" professor Stevens chuckled.

"Well, if all the others agree, there's going to be five of us, so about 40% sure", answered Adrian with a completely innocent face.

"You truly are something else at times, Mr. Milner. Very well, you boys go have your fun tomorrow. Just be prepared for a bunch of mocking comments from other high schools based on our losing streak."

"*I truly pity the existence of the people who would be foolish enough to try any mocking comments tomorrow...*" Steven thought to himself, remembering the interaction with the nosy girl from yesterday.

"*Really, these guys think they have any sort of shot at forming a successful band? They look like stick figure doodles from Saturday morning cartoons.*" a contemptuous classmate named Ryan thought to himself.

He was a person that lived for sneering and derisive remarks, which he sometimes muttered under his breath just loud enough for other people except teachers to hear.

He was also the classmate that Steven mentioned the other day to Dennis.

The bell then rang, signaling the end of the school day, as the math class, with a hint of homeroom teacher pep talk, was the last class of the day for Steven and Adrian.

As they stood up from their desks, packing their backpacks, Steven asked his brother:

"So, who's coming with us to this event again?"

"Those three over there, there, and there", replied Adrian, pointing Steven to Callum, Parker, and Jack. "I heard them say during yesterday's presentation period how they were into music, or studying music, or want to study music, or some combination between those three things."

"But do they know about our band idea?"

"Sort of. I asked them briefly this morning how they feel about the competition and they said they'd be willing to be part of a band. They haven't spoken with anyone else yet."

"I mean, they do seem nice. Jack's a tad more introverted so, you know, he'll fit right in with you. Parker seems very into music trivia and Callum...I can't help but feel he's the one we met when we dropped our admittance papers here."

"Yeah, he's the one, we went through that briefly as well earlier", Adrian said while putting the last of his notebooks in his backpack.

The twins then went and asked Callum, Parker and Jack if they wanted to join them tomorrow, and they were more than happy to. After all, it did in fact mean they could skip some classes without having to worry about disgruntled looks from teachers.

The presentation event

Early next morning, Steven and Adrian were both getting ready to leave for Michael Bryan Sanders High School. Since their house was closest to the bus station, they decided that everyone should meet there and they were going to leave together.

Sure enough, Callum, Parker, and Jack showed up just as the twins were ready to go.

As they arrived at the bus station, Adrian was deep in thought about something. Callum then leaned towards Steven, who was scrolling through the latest motorsport news, and whispered:

"So, anything odd we need to know about Adrian?"

"He speaks in a ton of musical references, which at this point is his first language, with English being second. He also manages to come up with deeply analytical insults whenever someone insults him first. And he firmly believes in the outside world, while also believing we're in a book."

"Or movie, or TV show, depending on the medium", added Adrian, still in a state of deep thought, but paying attention to the conversation.

"Wait, so you're like one of those comic book characters that does the whole breaking the fourth wall type of thing?" Callum asked, with genuine interest.

Adrian snapped out of his previous mood, looked at his brother with a rather smug look and said:

"Do you see that, dark-haired Rapunzel? That is how someone should react to such a revelation."

Steven gave his brother a bemused smirk.

"I'm not saying I believe you, it's just that it seems cool. Can you like...see into the future and find out what happens?" asked Callum.

"No, sadly. It would have been quite a dull story if I actually knew. You'll just have to settle for the odd remark and me questioning Millie's writing abilities."

"Who is Millie?" all three newcomers asked. Jack and Parker became curious about this conversation after it picked up some steam.

"Oh, the guy who writes these stories. Short for Milner, I believe."

"Wait, so you say we're in a book, and the author's name is Milner as well?" Callum asked with a slight disbelief in his voice.

"Yes. He's very creative with music, it seems, but names are above his pay grade."

Everyone had a good laugh about this conversation.

"I like to refer to this as glitching. He does this from time to time, so it's best to get used to it early", said Steven.

When the bus finally arrived, they boarded it and went to the top floor, as it was a double-decker.

Since it was quite silent in the bus, Adrian was able to take off his headphones, prompting Parker to ask:

"How do those things work anyway?"

"They have some filters in them that act as a noise gate and some forms of high-pass and low-pass filters where needed. Basically, they block certain sounds under a given volume level, and also lower the volume of sounds that are under or over certain pitches, from entering my ear."

"Why do you need them though?" asked Jack.

"I've had many doctors try to answer that very question. I didn't always need them, but something happened approximately four years ago. A few of our elementary school classmates changed schools and a few days before the event I started having these weird symptoms."

Adrian then took a short break to take a small drink of water.

"After about a month of various diagnoses, one doctor finally came up with the brilliant idea to give me...earplugs. Somehow it worked, and then we got in contact with someone that would be able to help us with creating these headphones. They allow me to hear the main...pitch of a voice, I guess? But you know, without the extra noise. And they're easier to handle than regular noise-cancelling ones."

"So, you can't really live without them for the moment?"

"I can, in areas where there's little ambient noise, like at home, the library, somewhat empty buses, and so on. It seems to be some form of misophonia, but like a mutated version that has its own mind or something, because it doesn't behave like it's supposed to."

"I am curious, what would happen if someone took them off?" asked Parker.

"If I knew it was coming? Nothing because I'd most likely block it. If someone tries to do it as a prank though, last time that happened, it sent me into a panic-induced moment of rage, that scared basically all of my classmates and in which I almost knocked out two of them with a single punch to the stomach each", answered Adrian with a bit of sadness in his voice.

After a brief moment of silence, he continued:

"So yeah, I'm not opposed to pranks, but if you're going to try out anything, stay away from these little things unless you tell me otherwise."

Steven noticed they arrived at their station and all of them got off the bus. After a five-minute walk, they finally reached their destination, Michael Bryan Sanders High School.

It's worth noting that in terms of education, Sanders High was the pride of the city. It had a vast courtyard, that featured a lot of green spaces for the students to relax, along with a large number of areas with trees that allowed anyone to cool off during hot summer days.

And in the middle of it, there was the main high school building, with the rehearsal building on its left and the gym and sports building on its right. The presentation event was going to take place in front of the main building, where a stage area was already in place.

The only aspect that ruined an otherwise perfectly elegant and beautiful place was the statue that was at the entrance of the courtyard.

"What a weird combination of various musical instruments and musical symbols. And the way they combine into a nightmare-inducing contraption that makes absolutely no sense is something else. Is this what the outsiders call computer generated slop?", Adrian thought to himself.

The boys settled in a somewhat empty area, where they could still hear themselves talk over the chatter around them. And there was quite a hefty amount of chatter.

"Uh, guys, did anyone read the fine-print on these competition rules?" asked Steven.

"Not in so much detail, why?" said Callum.

"It says here that in the event of two bands being tied in their final scoring, there is to be a deciding song that is going to be chosen at random from a list, before the competition."

"So basically, we have to write some original songs and also be prepared for a song duel, I guess? All that's missing is an animatronic raccoon, a green alien, a grey alien who can't help but be blunt, and a purple stone", added Callum.

"I mean, about the grey alien who can't help but be blunt..." said Steven, as Adrian was giving him a sarcastic stare.

"On that note, what genres or influences should we focus on? If we do end up in a band, what gives us the best chance at winning?" asked Parker.

"Good one. For the heavy metal side, anything that involves neo-classical elements is going to be cool and easy to create something epic from. However, if we want or need to do progressive or indie stuff, combining it into heavy metal is going to be a trip, though it might be worth a shot if the riffs are good", said Adrian.

"Yeah, and for punk, the easiest route to create something catchy is pop-punk, though I do enjoy some of that rage-filled punk rock quite a lot", said Steven.

"Oh man, I love pop-punk, we should definitely incorporate some elements from that area", added Callum.

"I'm quite partial to thrash metal and progressive", said Parker.

"I'm fine with any option, though with my classical guitar studies, I will probably want to look into that genre of music as well", said Jack.

The ceremony then finally began. After a long, drawn-out speech by Jessica Larson, the headmaster or principal of Sanders High, in which she made sure to highlight that her high school was currently on a five consecutive wins streak, she then invited a representative from each high school to say a few words.

First up was Brooks R. Hawkins High School, whose representative was a girl from Callum's elementary school days. Her speech was good, focusing on the efforts she and her band mates would be doing to ensure they were going to win.

Then, it was Richard B. Maddison Riverside High School, whose representative seemed to be a former colleague of Parker's. His speech contained a lot of water references for whatever reason, though studying next to a river probably had a lot to do with it.

And since headmaster Larson already did the grand speech in the beginning, it was now time for Andrew F. Gordon High School. Against Adrian's wishes, Steven got up and started walking towards the stage. He put his sunglasses on and as he was going down the lane towards the drawing area, he heard a number of jokes addressed at his high school's two decade long winless streak.

As he arrived on the stage, the headmaster said:

"I'm surprised Gordon High even has the guts to send students to this thing. Nevertheless, how does it feel to stand in the presence of greatness, mister..."

"Steven, professor. As for the greatness aspect, I see no mirror in which to reflect myself in, so I guess I should ask you to answer me the same question", said Steven, trying to keep his composure intact.

There was quite an audible gasp coming from the audience next to the stage. Adrian thought to himself: *"So when I get to tell this story to my kids, I can honestly begin with* Once upon a time, your uncle Steven shut everyone up..."

The headmaster herself was also a bit stunned by this remark. Steven seemed to have touched a bit of a nerve with what he said.

"I have to admit, mister Steven, this has been the best fight your minuscule high school has put up in years. I should know, I was present to every single one of your humiliating defeats in the last 18 years", said the headmaster through gritted teeth.

"Well then, that's horrible news for you. If I managed to get under your skin after only two days of high school, just imagine what our band is going to do to your ego after three years of practice", answered Steven, in a somewhat innocent tone.

"Unreal, it's like I'm channeling my thoughts to him. Is this the twin connection that movies and books keep trying to imply exists between twins?', Adrian thought to himself once more, his jaw dropping. The chatter and gasps around them were becoming louder by the minute.

Professor Larson was absolutely livid:

"Alright then Steven. Since you wanted greatness on stage, allow me to introduce you to a much more accomplished musician than you. Henry Adams, please come on stage."

Sure enough, Henry Adams was one of the people that Steven heard making rude comments earlier. Weirdly enough, his confidence seems to have left him when he ended up on stage.

"Now Henry, I am feeling quite generous today. Instead of me, the adult with much more life experience, telling Steven about our school's accomplishments, I am going to let you do it. So please, tell our guest how in over his head he actually is."

Henry looked at the audience, then at headmaster Larson, and then at Steven, who was completely unimpressed, and even took his sunglasses off so Henry could see he was not scared.

There was a bit of an awkward pause, as Henry could not find his words. Noticing this, headmaster Larson felt the need to intervene, to try and save face:

"Very kind of you Henry. Not wanting to make our guests feel ashamed. I am proud of you. You may return to the audience now."

After Henry left the stage, and before professor Larson could continue, Steven said:

"You know, these victories that you have in your head only exist there. You had very little to do with whatever successes this high school has had in the competition, if reports are anything to be believed. Unlike you, I did my research and some of your previous winners said that they took whatever advice you gave them and did the opposite. Because otherwise, they'd have lost, and badly."

To say headmaster Larson was even more livid would be the biggest understatement in history:

"Alright, mister loud mouth, I've had enough of this insolence. There is no possibility in this world or the mythical outside one that you actually win this competition. And just to show you that, I am going to give you the tie breaker song name right now, in front of everyone."

Steven raised his left eye-brow for a bit, but didn't say anything.

"Stunned into silence, finally? Good, your voice is grating to the ears. Now, take this song name, and get off my stage. The presentation is over. Everybody, go home, now!"

She then submitted a notification regarding the chosen song for Gordon High, while Steven took the note containing the song name and started walking silently and confidently, sunglasses back on, to his classmates.

"Pick your jaws up the floor, it's time to go", he said after reaching them.

The boys started walking, all the while wondering what had gotten into Steven all of a sudden. Once they left the courtyard though, Steven just started laughing.

"Oh man, did you see the look on the headmaster's face? Those moments are going to haunt her dreams for a good few months."

"Mate, what even was that? What...what were you doing?" asked everyone in disbelief.

"Oh right, I should probably explain. I have a good feeling that this competition was somewhat rigged in recent years. I've listened to the winners, and they were way below the other high school bands in terms of abilities. And I wanted to get us an advantage that is actually written in the rulebook for our competition. I made sure Jess wrote it and submitted it to the official rules and regulations platform."

Sure enough, upon verification, it showed up in the platform on their phones. Upon checking the name of the tie-breaker song, Steven asked his brother:

"So, how's your confidence?"

"Well, after seeing what song was thrust upon us, I can safely say she's gone, much like my inner voice after realizing how high you have to go in that song..."

A band is formed

On their way home, the five boys were engaged in a heated discussion about the day's events:

"Man, the face on that Jessica Larson woman when you told her the mirror bit", laughed Callum.

"I mean, I could have done a lot worse. I could have told her something along the lines of *the only one remotely connected to music on this stage is me, so you are right, I am in the presence of greatness*. Though that feels like something I have to earn first, in one way or another", said Steven.

"I feel like what you actually ended up saying was way worse for her. And on that note, I want to say I want to become part of the band", said Parker. "I know Adrian's the designated guitarist, so I'll go with drums, with the only request being that you don't completely ignore my songwriting ideas."

"I want to join in on that, too", said Jack. "I do love guitar, but I could go with being the bass player. But we would need to acquire a bass guitar somehow."

"That should be easily solved if we look for a used one, there's bound to be one lying around in this city of all places", said Adrian. "What about you, Callum?"

Callum thought for a bit.

"I mean, I want to join, but I'm not sure about being a lead singer and I don't currently own a guitar. My parents did say they'd be willing to buy me one should I want to join a band. They get their pay checks in about three weeks."

"That's cool. If anything, I could lend you my old electric guitar if you don't manage to get it in time", said Adrian.

With that being established, there was one giant elephant in the bus that needed to be addressed:

"So that leaves Steven as the lead singer then?" asked Parker.

"I suppose so. I will need to work on my voice a lot, but I suppose that can be accomplished. We have two entire school years to prepare for the first major test."

There was an air of anxious enthusiasm in the group. Neither one of them had ever played in a band before. The only one close to that was Adrian, who had some semblance of such moments during his guitar lessons.

The boys also came to the consensus and realization that sometimes, fights will occur because of clashing ideas, and they agreed that they would try to resolve it with as much maturity as possible. Threats to quit the band were not to be accepted and if there wasn't a majority agreement on a certain idea, they would not go ahead with it.

"We'll also probably need a name and a logo", added Adrian.

"Oh, I can work on the logo, no problem", said Callum.

"That's good. I'll also go more into learning about music production. I have the basics nailed down, but I need to work on making songs release-ready", said Adrian.

As the group was discussing potential band names, with ideas such as Riot Forge and Iron Vandal being tossed around, the bus had reached their station, so they got off.

They then bid farewell to one another and went home. On their way home, Adrian suggested a quick stop to The Multiverse Junction comic store, to which Steven agreed.

As they were entering the store, their classmate Ryan was just leaving. Upon seeing them, he made a snide remark:

"I see not-Thor and his wannabe motorcycle-riding brother have arrived to give us a show."

"Yes, I am terribly sorry I got the part instead of you", answered Adrian. "There might be an opening for screaming-extra-number-three if you're interested though. Which I assume you're not, since a man of your intellect and caliber would never be caught taking part in such nerdy activities, would he?"

"Oh, a comeback line, I'm shaking. Want to come and say it to my face?"

"I'm one foot away from you Ryan, any closer and we'd be exchanging body odor or other fluids. Which I also assume you're not interested in. Now, can you please move along? You're making a scene and it's making you uncomfortable."

"You mean...it's making you uncomfortable", said Ryan with a sneer.

"I know what I said", answered Adrian.

Seeing as Adrian was not impressed by his attitude, Ryan said with quite the bravado:

"Fine, I'll leave you two alone to discuss your ... ahem ... private thoughts. See you losers in class tomorrow, I'm going to go wash away the nerdy vibes."

After he left, Steven asked his brother:

"What's his deal? I heard some rude comments from him the other day as well."

"His older brother, I guess. He's obviously compensating for something, but I don't know what.

Seems to me he doesn't want people to know he's into comics or other non-cool activities."

The twins then went along and looked through the comics. Some variant covers caught Adrian's eye.

"Have you decided on anything?" asked Steven.

"Hm, I could take anything ... anything out of these three. I think I'll go with this one, the claws are way too good to pass on."

After paying for the comic book, the twins went home and ate lunch.

The next three weeks passed without many notable events. While Steven's antics with headmaster Larson made the rounds for a few days, the talk of the high school was soon replaced with more pressing manners, as students were scrambling around trying to form bands, streaming and discussing potential influences for their music.

And, perhaps even more importantly, everyone started getting ready for the Freshman Ball, which was to be held on the 15th of October, and was a really good place for students to get to know each other and, if they were lucky, even go there with a partner of their choosing.

However, before the Ball, Callum asked everyone to keep the 9th of October open, as he was ready to go and purchase his guitar. And as luck would have it, Jack also got into contact with someone who had an extra bass guitar for sale.

New and interesting instruments

Callum was so eager to buy his new guitar that he arrived at the Milner's house at 9 AM, 45 minutes before they were all supposed to meet.

He knocked on the door and was greeted by Mrs. Milner:

"Good morning. You must be Callum. Would you like a cup of tea?"

"Yes, please. Are Steven and Adrian up? I am a bit early."

"Adrian is still sleeping, curiously enough. Steven is in the living room. You can go there and I'll bring you your tea."

Callum went into the living room to find Steven looking at the ceiling with a very intense concentration.

"What are you looking at?"

"I have absolutely no idea, but it's one of the most intense things I've ever witnessed. Anyway, you're here early."

"Yeah, I just couldn't wait. I really want to go to the shop."

Mrs. Milner brought Callum his cup of tea and he started drinking it. After some discussions about the unfairness of math and math tests, Callum asked:

"Heard you two had a meeting with headmaster John Turner the other day. What was that about?"

"Oh, the Jessica Larson incident. Nothing bad, per se, headmaster Johnny just wanted to make sure we could back up the talk. So, you know, absolutely no pressure."

"Yeah, none at all", laughed Callum.

Upon finishing his drink, he continued:

"When do you think Adrian's going to wake up?"

"Well, he did say that if he's not up until 9:15, I should wake him up. And since it's 9:15, I think it's time I did."

The duo went to Adrian's room, and Steven made a sign with his finger towards Callum to keep quiet. Afterwards, he proceeded to start banging on his brother's door and shouting:

"Wake up you lazy bum, they're going to close the all-night-open stores if you don't move!"

After a few seconds, Adrian opened the door, his eyes barely open and his face that of a person who needed more sleep:

"Thanks for the subtle wake-up. Now, allow me a few minutes to get dressed", he said half-awake.

After getting dressed and having a bite to eat, the three of them were ready to go to the guitar shop. Soon after they left, Jack and Parker also arrived, with Jack saying that after they're done guitar shopping, they could go and meet the person that had an extra bass guitar for sale.

As they boarded the bus and sat down, a visibly confused and still tired Adrian asked:

"Did I talk to any of you guys on the phone last night? Like really late?"

"Oh yeah, I called you, telling you that today is the day I buy my guitar", answered Callum with a chuckle.

"Oh. That explains the sleeping-in part of this morning then."

After about 20 minutes, the boys were off the bus and on their way to the shop, which has located in in the city center area, close to Passaggio Park.

"So, what should one look for in a guitar?" asked Callum.

"Well, the safest option would be a Stratocaster-style one, as it's really comfortable and easy to play, but I can hear you falling asleep already. Since we're going to do heavy metal and punk, you'll want one that has humbucker-type pickups. You know, the thing that captures the sound of a string and transforms it into an electrical signal. But you want the type of guitar that has two sets of two of those things, with like two rows of magnets."

"Right, I think I know what you're referring to. Does the brand or type of these things matter or not?"

"Well, guitar snobs will say yes, however, tests conducted by an online content creator tell you that the difference in sound when using distorted guitars is minimal, so no, they don't. Dylan, the sales guy, will try to convince you to buy the more expensive ones because of the snob mentality. Do not buy into this, just smile, nod, and buy the guitar you like the most in terms of looks, pickup selector functionality, and number of frets if you really think you'll be using that 24th fret a lot."

With this in mind, the boys went into the shop. They were immediately welcomed with a barrage of riffs, some played well, some not, combined with the sound of tuning guitars and the beautiful and distinctive smell of guitars, amplifiers, complemented by disgruntled employee grunts, who were tired of hearing the aforementioned riffs over and over again.

Steven, Parker and Jack went off to look at random instruments, while Adrian and Callum started looking at guitars and amplifiers.

After scanning the available options for a bit, Callum was down to three options, out of which he chose one that resembled something called a flying-V shape in the outer world, popularized by a certain rhythm guitarist from Los Angeles.

"Hm, I think I'm going to with this one. It's very easy to play and given that it's not the classical flying V type and I can actually hold it on my leg, it's the best fit."

Adrian nodded in agreement and despite Dylan's best efforts to convince him how the more expensive option was better because of some weird, salesy claims about something or another, it was Callum's final answer.

After also settling on a 20W guitar combo amplifier that featured both clean and distorted channels, Callum was all set and ready to go.

"Guys", said Jack, "my friend with the bass lives about 10 minutes from there and he said we could meet him there when we're done." They decided to go, but only after stopping for a quick snack.

Upon arriving at Jack's friends' house, he was getting ready to leave for a doctor's appointment, but still had a few spare minutes:

"Follow me guys, the guitar is here", said the friend whose name was Mark, leading them to his room.

After laying eyes on the bass guitar prize, the boys were a bit in disbelief:

"I mean, Mark did say it has a bit of an unconventional paint job", said Jack.

"I'm not sure you can change the font color of texting apps, but if it's still possible, this is the shade I'm using from now on", added Parker.

"You know, the outsiders have a song called Barbie Girl that would fit the vibe of this song really well", an amused Adrian noted.

"Come on guys, this is the most beautiful piece of music instruments I've ever seen. I mean, if you slap a pink wig on your head and wear a very round ear-ring, it's the perfect crossover cosplay, at least according to some weird tales Adrian keeps harping on about from the outside world", said Steven, who was actually being honest about his opinion.

"Guys, I don't mean to be a rude host, but I do have to leave for my doctor's appointment. Is it yay or nay?" asked Mark.

"I'm pretty confident we have an over-enthusiastic yay, a couple of reluctant ones, a *meh, I'm not playing it so I don't care* and someone who's questioning his life and friendship choices", said Adrian.

"Like he already mentioned, I did tell Jack it's an unconventional color, this bass."

Jack gave Mark a long hard stare and laughed a bit, and in the end, they all agreed to purchase the instrument. They all chipped in with 30 Cantors each, as Mark was willing to lower his price if it meant he could sell the instrument.

Note that a Cantor was the national currency of Canterevia, and its value, if we were to associate it with something from the outside world, was somewhere between one USD and one EUR.

With all their instruments issues solved (Parker was to use the drumkit at the high school rehearsal room and whatever air drumming techniques he could find until he bought some electronic ones for home practice), the boys then boarded the bus for the ride home.

After a few minutes, Callum asked:

"So, did any of you guys land a date for the Freshman Ball?"

"Nope", said Parker.

"Me neither", added Jack.

"Didn't even bother to try", said Steven.

"Yeah, I didn't get one either. What about you Adrian?"

Adrian contemplated for a bit and answered:

"I think I managed to get something worse than a no."

"What do you mean?" asked the others.

"Well, I asked Imogen, and her answer was something along the lines of *well, we'll both be going, so I guess we'll see each other there in some way or another*. So, you know, I won't be going with you, but since you'll probably be coming, you'll get to see who I went along with."

The other four boys were left stunned by this answer. After a few minutes of silence, Steven hugged his brother, right before handing him a scrambled three-by-three Rubik's Cube. Adrian was very thankful of this gesture.

"So, you're still going to go, even after that?" asked Callum.

"Yeah. I mean, I've already been rejected so the worst part of it is out the window. And even if something embarrassing happens to one of you, you'll at least get to say *well, at least I wasn't Adrian trying to ask Imogen to the Freshman Ball*."

Everyone laughed at this remark and the boys were in good spirits once again.

Little did Adrian know though, the Freshman Ball was about to test his beliefs and principles in a way that he wasn't expecting.

Freshman Ball reconciliation

The week of the Freshman Ball passed by like how a hypercar passes the original Mulsanne straight in our world. Adrian and Steven were not exactly in high spirits over the upcoming event.

Truthfully though, only Adrian was feeling down, Steven was just curious what all the fuss was about.

The five band members agreed to start rehearsing next week so as to have the Ball pass and to give Parker enough time to install his electronic drum kit, which had a delay in its delivery.

After the final classes on Friday, the twins went home and played around on their console for a bit. Then it was time to get ready, an activity which Steven revelled in for the most part. He liked to take his time in front of a mirror.

Adrian decided to trade his usual grey t-shirt for an even greyer shirt, which was the only thing that he and his mother managed to compromise on. There was to be no budging on the jeans though, as Adrian concluded he was already uncomfortable enough by being there after the whole debacle with his classmate Imogen.

After eating a bit for supper, their father drove them to the club where the Freshman Ball was taking place, called Harmony House, where they met up with their friends.

"Ah, I see you're looking...the same but with a shirt", noted Callum when he saw the twins arrive.

"Very shrewd of you", said Adrian with a sarcastic tone.

"Now, now, let's not fight. I have a sinking feeling we don't need more attention on us than what is required. Which is basically just saying our name to the bouncer and getting in", noted Steven.

And in they went, all five of them. Upon entering, they were met with some admittedly very nice synthpop tunes. There were some designated booth areas, where the boys went to the one they reserved, and a very large dance floor, which was already starting to get filled by other students.

The light show was pretty colorful and it gave the whole place a very upbeat and partylike mood. Adrian put on his headphones and was enjoying the synth sounds he was hearing, trying to visualize them in terms of waveforms and ADSR envelopes.

This activity allowed him to unwind quite a bit, as he ordered himself a soft drink.

"You know, I heard some people mention something about trying to smuggle in some beers and other alcoholic drinks. Any of you interested?" asked Parker.

"Not really, and given our mom's incredible sense of smell, I don't think it's a really good idea", said Steven.

"I agree. And besides, alcohol is way too overrated. Seriously, I think it's the same thing to fun as drop tunings are to metal", added Adrian.

"Oh, do expand, please", said Parker.

"It's like…if the only way you can have any sort of fun is with alcohol, then you're not really capable of having fun. Similarly, if you can't sound heavy without down tuning your guitar to a bass, then you can't sound heavy."

The other four boys were actually impressed with this analogy.

"Seriously, I'm half-expecting that someday, tunings will get so low, they'll hit the brown note. And the artist that does that will have invented a new genre. Check out the latest trend called Brown Note Metal. It will set you free in ways you never imagined." added Adrian with a radio-like voice.

Everyone laughed at this idea and Parker said:

"You know, I tend to agree with you. I think alcohol would actually ruin you. The fact that you can come up with these absurdities in your natural state is a sight to behold."

Adrian then mimicked taking a bow.

Jack then noticed that next to the dance floor, there was a stage.

"Think we're getting some live music as well?" he asked.

"Yeah, I did hear something about that, supposedly some band that started in this town and made it big. Venom Spire is their name, I believe", said Callum.

The group agreed that it was quite a good name for a band that. Adrian, having finished his drink, suggested they go next to the dance floor, to see what was going on in that area as well. The boys got up just as Steven's drink also arrived. He ordered it after Adrian got his.

"You guys go ahead. I'll catch up with you in a bit."

"I mean, you could always take your drink with you, you know", his brother mentioned.

"I would but...have you felt these couches? They're extraordinarily comfortable."

Adrian shook his head and laughed a bit, then went on with the other three.

As Steven was sat at his table and looked around, he noticed a familiar figure. It was none other than the obnoxious girl from their first day of high school.

She seemed to be in an intense discussion with another boy, who was unimpressed by whatever she was saying. After a while, the boy just turned his back and went on his way, leaving the girl completely dumbfounded.

"That poor girl can't catch a break...", Steven thought to himself.

The girl was completely dismayed and she started looking around, as if desperately looking for something or someone that she could talk to.

Steven was busy with his drink when he noticed she started walking his way. He of course did not forget their first day encounter, but something wasn't allowing him to walk away.

After a few seconds, she was at their booth and, with a bit of a tremble in her voice, started talking:

"Listen, I know I have a lot of nerve coming here and there are fewer people you'd probably want to see less than me right now, but...I just have literally no one to go to right now. My friend couldn't make it to the Ball, and I'm all alone, and-"

"Sorry to interrupt, but if this is some form of sob story to get me impressed, I wanted to kindly let you know that I am fairly oblivious to this kind of stuff. However, I did notice you did have a bit of a run-in with someone, and I assume your sadness is real so...you can stop now and it's fine?", said Steven, quite unsure how this would come off.

The girl's trembling voice became a lot calmer:

"Heh, thanks. It's alright, I just...first off, sorry for our first day encounter. I was rude, I was brash, I honestly don't know what was in my mind. I've been trying to muster up the courage to say this for a few weeks now but didn't know how to do it. Apparently, like-a-band-aid is a good enough approach."

"No worries, at least from my side. My brother might take a bit more convincing though, but we'll cross that bridge when we meet it, which now that I think about it, should have been two minutes ago."

"And why is that?"

As this conversation was going on, Adrian and the boys were next to the dancefloor, each trying to figure out if they should start dancing or not. The music was good enough, but their dancing skills were less than ideal.

As they each tried to convince one another to go first, Adrian noted:

"What exactly is Steven doing? Judging by his usual drinking rate, he should have finished his drink about two minutes ago."

"You know how fast people drink?" asked Parker in disbelief.

"I can instantly figure out the pitch of every word you speak, do something called fourth-wall-breaking when I feel like it, can probably name every guitar released in any given year, and this is what freaks you out the most?" asked Adrian.

"I mean...wait, what is that about each guitar released in any given year?"

"Yeah, basically, if you give me any year, I can tell you every guitar make and model released, and..." started Adrian, but suddenly stopped. "Oh, for the love of Avenged Sevenfold's 2007 self-titled album from the outside world, what is Steven doing?" he continued with a visibly annoyed voice.

"It's called talking to a girl. You'll get there someday too", said Jack in an amused tone.

Adrian gave him a death stare and then continued:

"It's not that. That girl is an obnoxious being that we butted heads with during our first day of high school."

"What'd she do, call you a mommy's boy?" asked Parker, laughing a bit.

"Well...yes, exactly that."

"So? It's very obvious you are one."

"Of course it's obvious Parker, and you melon heads poking fun at it is no issue, but using it as an insult is something I will never tolerate. Our parents went through a lot of hardships trying to provide us with the best life possible. They were almost homeless at one point. And my guitar, that I built with my dad? He said it was for our bonding, but truthfully, it was due to lack of money to purchase a new one, or even a used one. And if it wasn't for him knowing a luthier, even that would have been a stretch. I never told him that because I enjoyed the process of creating a guitar from scratch, but you'll excuse me if I don't allow strangers to badmouth my parents."

Taken aback by this revelation, Parker apologized:

"Sorry, I wasn't aware of this."

"Well, I do not generally advertise it because I hate pity looks and if anyone of you dares to change your attitude or stop your funny little jabs at my quirks because of it, I don't want you in the band. This is just something you should know, and if possible, never mention again. Is that clear?"

"Duly noted. But why is it an issue if Steven talks to that girl?"

"Because, in my foolish naivety, I was hoping to go the next four years of high school without having to interact with her again. And Steven always has this ability to see the best in people and make friends with almost anyone, most especially with people that annoy me. I can name at least three or four people from elementary school which annoyed me to the best of their abilities that became some of our best friends during that time."

"I don't see it as that big of an issue since they became best friends of yours. On the plus side, it's funny seeing you like this. Just proves my alcohol-would-make-you-worse theory correct."

"Your elementary school class mate Ryan wants to see me cry, you like seeing me annoyed. What sort of experimenting did they do to you in that cursed building?"

"We're ... not allowed to talk about it", said Parker with an obviously exaggerated mysterious tone.

As the two were having this intense conversation, Steven and the girl made their way to them.

"You say that if I hold my own in terms of wit, it's going to be fine?" she asked, a bit unsure.

"Yes. Adrian is never going to admit it, but I am four for four in terms of people that annoy him that then became our friends because of my meddling. Just be your witty self, don't insult our parents or his guitar, not even as a joke, and you'll be fine. Also, make sure your comebacks have some sort of musical element in them."

As the two arrived near the dance floor, Parker and Jack took a step back, ready to enjoy what was undoubtedly going to be a good show.

"Well, if it isn't the actual source of inspiration for horror movie soundtracks..." a miffed Adrian noted, with his hands crossed over his chest.

"Well, first off, I apologize to you as well for my outburst during our last encounter. And I ... uhm ... I figured I would fit right in with the guy who ... uhm ... probably had some of his grunts and sighs put in those movies as well", the girl answered, her voice quivering a bit.

Parker and Jack could barely contain their laughter. Adrian uncrossed his hands and squinted a bit. He was curious about the newcomer's abilities.

"I see someone listened to female empowerment songs today and decided she's going to show the world a thing or two."

"This is rich, coming from someone who probably secretly enjoys those songs just as much as their intended audience."

Adrian started smiling after this retort, but it wasn't a smile of contempt. Rather, he was quite impressed with the girl's humor. Parker and Jack on the other hand were laughing out loud.

"I'm legitimately impressed. You held your own for two straight quips, which is a new record. Though, with the previous one actually being, well, one, it's more of a participation trophy."

"Maybe you can print me a diploma, and put a copy next to your musical trivia games high scores accomplishments."

"That would require you give me your name. Or should I go with *bothersome-pop-punk-schoolmate*?"

"Whatever works for you", the girl said, with a slightly less confident voice.

"Nah, nah, wait a minute. Your voice changed. There's something there, there's definitely something there..." Adrian said, noticing the voice change.

"I just don't think we're ready to be on a first-name basis yet", added the girl, trying to maintain a cool composure.

Adrian was having none of this:

"What's your name, girl?"

After a few seconds, she muttered under her breath:

"Avril".

"Av-what?"

"It's Avril, ok? Avril Lawson", the girl added with a somewhat defeated yet exasperated voice.

Adrian nodded his head in a slow motion and said:

"See, was that so hard? No reason to go out of your way to make things complicated."

Avril rolled her eyes, since it was clearly not the first time she ever heard this joke, which, as you might expect, originates from people claiming they know about the outside world.

It was quite evident she was smiling though. The tension was all but relieved and the first day encounter was put behind them. Adrian would never admit it, but he always trusted Steven's abilities to see the good in people.

"Did I miss anything?" Callum asked, appearing seemingly out of nowhere, after having disappeared for a few minutes.

"A lot. Where have you even been these last ten minutes?" asked Adrian.

"Oh, I had to use this club's facilities for...you know, something not very pleasant smelling."

Adrian then looked up and said, in a very defeated voice:

"This is going to be my life for the next four years."

Steven then hugged his brother for comfort, while the others just had a good laugh.

The rest of the night went on without anything notable happening, aside from the live act which started shortly after the reconciliation. Steven caught a glimpse of the theatrics and showmanship on display and was instantly hooked.

While everyone was busy either dancing, singing, or, in Adrian's case, trying to notice anything he could about live music setup with the help of Parker, Steven was completely mesmerized by the stage presence of the band.

The lead singer even noticed it and called him closer. They were in the middle of cover song and the singer asked Steven to sing a few notes into the microphone with him. A wobbly, but strangely melodic voice came out of Steven, who managed to keep his cool for an entire verse, to the approval of the lead singer.

Adrian noticed this moment as well and was fairly convinced that the band they had formed had all the right people in all the right places.

Now, it was only a matter of practice...and finding a vocal coach for Steven. And what no one knew at that time is that the vocal coach in question was closer to them than they thought.

Steven's new vocal coach

With the Freshman Ball behind them, Steven, Adrian and the others were finally ready to start rehearsals. They managed to find some suitable rehearsal hours, which were Mondays, Wednesdays and Thursdays at 2PM, right after school. Each band had their reserved slots in which they could practice and practice sessions were two hours long.

Andrew F. Gordon High School had a dedicated rehearsal room, equipped with everything required to play rock, punk, and metal music. There were three guitar amplifiers, and also two bass amps. And of course, there was a drumkit that occupied about half the length of the actual stage they were meant to play on.

The room was treated sonically so as to not disturb other students or classes should bands start rehearsing during school hours. Rehearsals were open to the public, unless the band currently in session hung a *Do Not Disturb* sign, in which case students were kindly asked not to enter, though not all of them abided by this rule.

The first week of rehearsals was a bit slow, because everybody was still getting up to speed with being in high school, being in a band, and abiding by Adrian's rule list, which consisted of one rule: don't be late.

This led to some arguments, as everybody was trying to get their point across to others, but not everyone was willing to listen. Luckily though, the arguments themselves were never serious, at least for now, and were usually resolved nicely after the rehearsal sessions, usually with a trip to a food truck or a cafeteria.

After the first week, Adrian noticed that some terms he was using, related to music production, were a bit confusing to his fellow bandmates, so he decided to make a list explaining what ADSR envelopes, double-tracking, vocal doubling, and many others, mean.

When passing along the list to everyone, Parker noted:

"I love the fact that you decided to be honest in the title of this list."

"What do you mean?"

"What do you mean what do I mean? You named the list *Adrian's alien-to-English music translation.*"

"Oh, that was my idea. I had Callum call him so he'd leave his work unattended, then I printed a list for each of us, so he wouldn't notice", said Steven.

"Doesn't that also make you an alien?" asked Adrian.

"Maybe, but maybe not. Maybe I fought against my programming and won."

"You really need to lay off the comics for a while", said Adrian.

After about a month of rehearsals, two things became clear. The first was that somehow, Adrian was in contention for Valedictorian, even though it was early days still. The second, more important one, was that Steven was in need of a vocal coach, because he was starting to hit his limit in the upper register of his voice. And during rehearsals, there were many a times when he had to go an octave lower on some notes. The good thing though is that he was able to tell when he was off pitch, regardless of the note height.

As they were getting ready for Thursday's rehearsal, Steven noticed that there was a band already practicing before them (they got off early from their final class). This wasn't usually the case, which meant that there was an updated schedule.

When Adrian arrived, he was surprised to hear a girl as lead singer. So far, they only heard boys as lead singers in every other band so this was a welcome change of scenery.

"Oh, I want to see who's playing", said Steven as he approached the door.

"Wait, we can't just burst in", noted Adrian.

"But there's no sign hung up. And you know what that means...free live music!"

"Fine, just let them finish their song first."

After finishing what proved to be quite a good rendition of a pop-punk song about small things, the twins entered the rehearsal room, only to find that it was none other than Avril Lawson as the lead singer.

"Oh, goody, just who I needed to un-brighten my day", commented Adrian.

When noticing the boys enter, Avril asked her bandmates:

"You forgot to put up the sign, didn't you?"

"Well, he was supposed to put it up", stated the lead guitarist pointing towards the bass player.

"No, he was supposed to put it up", blurted Van the bassist while pointing towards the guitarist.

"Stop lying", said Dan the guitarist.

"I'm not lying, you just forgot to put it up and are now putting the blame on me", replied Van.

"I didn't even know such a sign existed", remarked Sam the drummer.

Avril watched this unfold with bemusement on her face. Realizing that what is done is done, she turned towards the boys and said:

"Well. I guess I'm stuck with you as spectators now. Do be so kind as to keep quiet so as to not disturb us. We have...some situations."

Adrian and Steven chuckled and took a seat.

Once the blame game was over, Avril's band, still nameless by this point, started playing a heavy metal song.

Adrian decided to take this opportunity to study their local competition. Guitar-wise, Avril was doing an amazing job as rhythm guitarist, given the fact that she was also supposed to sing. Adrian was quite impressed by her chops and realized that should the band become fully functional in all areas, they would be quite the terrific adversary.

Steven on the other hand was mesmerized by Avril's voice and mannerisms on stage. He had this weird feeling in his stomach while watching her sing, it was something he never quite felt before. And to be fair, between her well controlled raspy vocals and amazing, almost metronome-like rhythm playing, you'd be wondering who wouldn't be amazed at such a display.

After finishing the song, Avril took a bow and told the boys that they could get ready as this was their final song of the day.

Adrian started getting things ready for him and Callum on guitars. Steven on the other hand had something else on his mind. He knew he had a lot to learn in terms of singing and he knew he needed a teacher. However, finding a professional one would probably imply quite the financial strain, as he was starting basically from scratch.

Noticing that he had an opening when Avril was coming down the stage, he blurted out the following question in one breath:

"Hey Avril, what would it take for me to convince you to teach me how to sing?"

Adrian was testing his tremolo bridge and almost broke one of his strings when he heard this.

Taken aback by this proposition, she looked at him a bit amazed:

"Um, sorry? You'd like for me to teach you how to sing? That sort of goes against the whole point of this being a competition you know."

"Yes, I do, but it's…it's weird, I…don't know many people who can sing like that. I mean, I have heard professional singers, but I never met one and…I don't know, I just want to learn how to sing exactly like you do. And...I guess I like it when you're around me."

Avril was even more confused, but she did appreciate the compliments:

"Thanks, I suppose. I never had anyone compliment my singing before. Nor have I had anyone say they like being around me. Usually, they just tolerate me and can't wait for me to leave the room."

"*I can attest to that, though you have become more tolerable as of late. Which is good news, considering where this is going...*", Adrian, who was listening to this exchange, thought to himself.

"Don't mention it. Adrian did a good job in helping me learn guitar, but singing is a bit out of his expertise. And every time he said he'll learn how to sing, he usually gets hung up in solving some weird mystery, either made up or based on something he learned", added Steven, his heart beating a bit faster and the feeling in his stomach growing ever more intense.

"Yeah, I can imagine tha-did you say mysteries?" asked Avril, a bit scared.

"Yeah, like he reads some plot points from a detective book and tries to solve it on his own. He says it keeps him busy and helps train his mind."

Upon hearing this, Avril became a bit skeptical. She was worried Adrian would start digging into her past. And while she wanted to say yes to Steven's proposition, she wanted to clear this up first.

Noticing that Parker and the others were entering the room, she knew she had little time to do so, but she wanted to do it right now so as to give Steven an answer. She asked him to give her a minute.

Then she approached Adrian, who was still busy connecting guitars and pedals:

"So, your brother wants me to teach him vocals and says you like mysteries."

"I heard, and yes, I do like mysteries. What of it?"

"I too like mysteries and detective books, and I know how inquisitive minds work, they want to solve every little riddle or conundrum they find and-"

"I am many things Avril, but stupid is not one of them. I am not going to dig up your past", interrupted Adrian so as to not let the others overhear anything.

The relief in Avril's expression was apparent. Thanking Adrian, she went back to Steven, who was eagerly awaiting an answer:

"What was that about?" he asked.

"I just wanted to gloat to your brother that I'm going to be spending a lot of time with you in order to teach you how to sing. And I wanted him to hear it from me."

"Yay, that's awesome!" an overjoyed Steven answered.

"We're going to figure out a schedule for learning vocals at school, as my place would make it a bit weird, and my father's interrogation techniques are not something you're ready for. I'll let you know what I come up with and we go from there. My main rule is simple, don't be late when we schedule a learning session", she added.

Steven was alright with this idea and after saying goodbye to everyone, Avril left and went home. She was not entirely sure what made her instantly agree to teaching Steven how to sing, but after analyzing it for a bit, she realized that being around him made her feel good and appreciated for once. And aside from her classmate Roxanne, he and Adrian were the only two who she could call her friends in the entire high school.

Callum's pop-punk anthem

Christmas was fast approaching and Steven and Adrian's band was gelling together quite well. Although the occasional creative sparks lead to some heated discussions regarding the direction of the band, the boys managed to keep it together and not let it affect their friendship or their work.

So far, they've only been rehearsing cover songs. Adrian was aware that other bands had already started working on original songs, and this was weighing on him, as he had a very distinct timeline which he hoped they would be able to follow.

However, he decided to let things happen for a while, without intervening, even though it made him twitch at times. With Christmas break on the horizon though, the lack of any original material was starting to worry him more and more. And it wasn't for lack of trying, but so far, they didn't manage to come up with something awe-inspiring.

"Are you still convinced you are alright with how things are going so far?" Steven asked him, as they were getting ready for one of their final rehearsal sessions before winter break.

"I am. I mean, I think I am. I mean … you know how in the past I always stepped in time when things needed a push in the right direction? I'll know when the time is right", answered Adrian.

"It'd help if you weren't twitching when you said that", remarked Avril, who decided to tag along for their rehearsal as well, to see how Steven's voice had improved in a live session setting.

"Yes, it probably would. I'll work on it."

As he put the finishing touches to the amp settings, Callum stormed into the room, almost out of breath.

"Let it … phew … be known that … agh … I was on time."

"Two minutes early, even. I know I said I hate people being late but you don't have to do this. We all know it's a long walk from our classroom two floors up to here", chuckled Adrian.

"Yeah, I know that, I usually end up being late because Steven is thoroughly amused by your reactions", said Callum while laughing and catching his breath.

Adrian looked at his brother with a satirical look on his face, and his response was to wave innocently at him.

"Anyway, what's the rush?" asked Adrian.

"You know, I'd tell you, but I'd rather show you."

He then plugged his guitar into the amp and started playing the following riff:

```
E|----------------|---------------------|
B|----------------|---------------------|
G|----------------|---------------------|
D|----------------|---------------------|
A|-7-7-7-7-7-7-7-7-|-9-9-9-11-11-11-9-9-|
E|-0-0-0-0-0-0-0-0-|-0-0-0-0--0--0--0-0-|


E|----------------|-------------------------|
B|----------------|-------------------------|
G|----------------|-------------------------|
D|----------------|-------------------------|
A|-9-9-9-9-9-9-9-9-|-11-11-11-12-12-12-11-11-|
E|-7-7-7-7-7-7-7-7-|-7--7--7--7--7--7--7--|


E|-------------------------|--------------------|
B|-------------------------|--------------------|
G|-------------------------|--------------------|
D|-------------------------|--------------------|
A|-11-11-11-11-11-11-11-11-|-9-9-9-11-11-11-9-9-|
E|-9--9--9--9--9--9--9--9--|-9-9-9-9--9--9--9-9-|
```

```
E | ----------------- | ----------------- |
B | ----------------- | ----------------- |
G | ----------------- | ----------------- |
D | ----------------- | ----------------- |
A | -7-7-7-7-7-7-7-7- | -9-9-9-7-7-7-6-7- |
E | -5-5-5-5-5-5-5-5- | -5-5-5-5-5-5-5-5- |
```

After playing the riff for two times, Callum stopped, wanting to see everyone's reaction.

Steven and Avril nodded in agreement towards Callum, while Jack and Parker, who just arrived, only caught a glimpse of it and weren't certain what it was.

Adrian on the other hand was mesmerized and fully focused on what he just heard:

"That's it", he whispered. "Play it again", he then added.

Callum then played it again and Adrian went a little bit closer to see what exactly he was playing. He was fairly certain he got it from the first iteration, but he wanted to be sure his 10 years of guitar and perfect pitch weren't for nothing.

After hearing it again, Adrian asked:

"Where'd you get this idea from?"

"Well, I started listening to some pop-punk bands. My folks are always going on and on about that sound and how good it was. I decided to give it a try, and after a healthy dose of listening, I managed to come up with this bad boy."

Adrian nodded. It was obvious he was in deep thought, as it had all the potential of making up an anthemic song if done right. Luckily for him, Parker put his thoughts into words:

"Dude, that riff is a thing of beauty, but is it exactly what we would need as an original, given our allotted sources of inspiration in terms of sound? Especially if we're in this thing to win it. I'm not sure the judges will be too lenient in that regard."

"Winning is good and all, but do we really want to pass this up as a potential song? We've tried tens if not hundreds of ideas in this past month and a half and this is the only time I remember all of us being in agreement, silent or spoken. We have something that can become a great song. I can already picture this being either a love song or...I don't know, something that should evoke a big moment in our lives", added Steven.

Parker gave those words a bit of thought, but in the end, he agreed with what Steven was saying.

"I'm open to working on it. Seems like the type of song with an easy bass line, too, just doubling the root note of whatever chord is playing", said Jack.

"So that's three, well, four, given that Callum would automatically be in agreement. So, what say you, lead guitarist?" asked Parker.

Adrian's mind was working at lightning speed, thinking about all the ways this song could go. He raised his index finger, asking for a minute of silence, while he put his thoughts together. After a while, he finally said:

"This isn't going to be a love song. This is going to be our graduation song. And even if we don't win, this song is going to be played at every graduation in Monodia for decades. As for the genre and all that nonsense, don't worry. We'll toss a solo in it, and bam, punk-rock song, it'll work. Mind if I give this a try?" he asked Callum.

"Yeah, sure thing", an enthusiastic Callum said.

Adrian took to the stage and kept fiddling around with the riff for a bit, trying to figure out where this was going as a song. After a few tries, he managed to come up with a follow up section to Callum's riff, that looked like this:

```
E | ----------------- | ----------------- |
B | ----------------- | ----------------- |
G | ----------------- | ----------------- |
D | ----------------- | ----------------- |
A | -7-7-7-7-7-7-7-7- | -7-7-7-7-7-7-7-7- |
E | -0-0-0-0-0-0-0-0- | -0-0-0-0-0-0-0-0- |
```

```
E |----------------|----------------|
B |----------------|----------------|
G |----------------|----------------|
D |-9-9-9-9-9-9-9-9-|-9-9-9-9-9-9-9-9-|
A |-9-9-9-9-9-9-9-9-|-9-9-9-9-9-9-9-9-|
E |-7-7-7-7-7-7-7-7-|-7-7-7-7-7-7-7-7-|


E |----------------|----------------|
B |----------------|----------------|
G |----------------|----------------|
D |-7-7-7-7-7-7-7-7-|-7-7-7-7-9-9-7-7-|
A |-7-7-7-7-7-7-7-7-|-7-7-7-7-9-9-7-7-|
E |-5-5-5-5-5-5-5-5-|-5-5-5-5-7-7-5-5-|


E |----------------|----------------|
B |----------------|----------------|
G |----------------|----------------|
D |-2-2-2-2-2-2-2-2-|-2-2-2-2-2-2-2-2-|
A |-2-2-2-2-2-2-2-2-|-2-2-2-2-2-2-2-2-|
E |-0-0-0-0-0-0-0-0-|-0-0-0-0-0-0-0-0-|
```

```
E|----------------|----------------|
B|----------------|----------------|
G|----------------|----------------|
D|-9-9-9-9-9-9-9-9-|-9-9-9-9-9-9-9-9-|
A|-9-9-9-9-9-9-9-9-|-9-9-9-9-9-9-9-9-|
E|-7-7-7-7-7-7-7-7-|-7-7-7-7-7-7-7-7-|


E|----------------|----------------|
B|----------------|----------------|
G|----------------|----------------|
D|-7-7-7-7-7-7-7-7-|-7-7-7-7-7-7-7-7-|
A|-7-7-7-7-7-7-7-7-|-7-7-7-7-7-7-7-7-|
E|-5-5-5-5-5-5-5-5-|-5-5-5-5-5-5-5-5-|


E|-----------------|-----------------|
B|-----------------|-----------------|
G|-----------------|-----------------|
D|-9-9-9-9-9-9-9-9-|-9-9-9-9-9-9-9-9-|
A|-9-9-9-9-9-9-9-9-|-9-9-9-9-9-9-9-9-|
E|-7-7-7-7-7-7-7-7-|-7-7-7-7-7-7-7-7-|
```

```
E|----------------|----------------|
B|----------------|----------------|
G|----------------|----------------|
D|----------------|----------------|
A|-7-7-7-7-7-7-7-7-|-7-7-7-7-7-7-7-7-|
E|-0-0-0-0-0-0-0-0-|-0-0-0-0-0-0-0-0-|

E|----------------------|------------------------|
B|----------------------|------------------------|
G|----------------------|------------------------|
D|----------------------|------------------------|
A|-11-11-11-11-11-11-11-11-|-11-11-11-11-11-11-11-11-|
E|-0--0--0--0--0--0--0--|-0--0--0--0--0--0--0--0--|
```

The song then leads back to the original riff, which was now the verse riff, with Adrian's addition being the chorus. And if there were any doubts beforehand, they were all but gone now. This was to become a song.

Jack even suggested the idea of having a pre-chorus after second verse section. Callum then thought for a bit and came up with this idea:

```
E|----------------|----------------|
B|----------------|----------------|
G|-7-7-7-7-7-7-7---|----------------|
D|-7-7-7-7-7-7-7-7-|-7-7-7-7-7-7-7-7-|
A|-5-5-5-5-5-5-5-7-|-7-7-7-7-7-7-7-7-|
E|--------------5-|-5-5-5-5-5-5-5-5-|
```

played 3 times and then

```
E | ----------------- | ----------------- |
B | ----------------- | ----------------- |
G | -7-7-7-7-7-7-7--- | ----------------- |
D | -7-7-7-7-7-7-7-9- | -9-9-9-9-9-9-9-9- |
A | -5-5-5-5-5-5-5-9- | -9-9-9-9-9-9-9-9- |
E | ---------------7- | -7-7-7-7-7-7-7-7- |
```

And with that section leading into the next chorus, they now had everything they needed to work on this song. Avril had the inspiration to go and put up the Do Not Disturb sign, but there was no way she was leaving just yet. After all, the twins still owed her a spectator session from before.

With everyone pumped up and ready to practice, they decided to try and see if they could come up with some ideas for the song. Ideas were flying faster than anyone had anticipated, so Avril agreed to try and write them down as soon as possible.

There were many good ideas that came about, and some really out-of-the-box ones, with Callum suggesting to add some artillery during some sections. Sadly though, the idea was scrapped as there were no cannons readily available for recording, supposedly due to a previous incident. No one knew what it was, but they were all intrigued and vowed to research it at some point.

Finally, after about 90 minutes of practicing and idea gathering, they had their list, which went something like this:

1. Song to start off with riff and vocals

2. Each verse section would have two verses

3. Bass to come in at the second verse

4. Drums to come in during chorus, but lightly at first

5. Full drums to come in during interlude between chorus and second verse section

6. Second chorus to feature lead guitar played over the chorus riff; debating on whether or not to add clean guitars

7. Solo to be played over verse riff after second chorus

8. One more chorus to be played after the solo and then the song ends

9. Fills and additional instruments to be discussed and added as song production progresses

"Well, I'm spent", said Adrian as he sat down at the edge of the stage.

"Me too. It's definitely the first time we've all agreed on something and actually worked in the same direction. More of this please", added Callum as he laid down next to Adrian.

The only one seemingly still in songwriting mode was Steven. He asked Avril for her pen and paper and started writing something while humming a melody line:

It's alright
Perfectly normal to feel fright
Wondering where friendships will go now
Getting ready to take a bow

You smile
Trying hard to keep your composure
Thinking of the things that need closure
Ready to travel the next mile

"*There's my star student...he finally seems to have a grasp on lower pitches*", Avril thought to herself, feeling quite proud.

The boys also agreed that the lyrics were good and that the vocal melody was perfect for the tune. Parker then asked Steven:

"Think you can sing that, but like...an octave higher or something?"

"Not at this moment in time I can't. I mean, I can reach higher notes, but I cap off at...uhm...what was that note again?"

"A4", said Adrian.

"That, yeah. And with this song, I'd have to go at...Adrian?"

"B4, at the very least."

"B4, apparently. Which at the moment is not something that can be achieved without a vicious attack on my private parts, which is not something I want to be a part of, for obvious reasons."

Everyone laughed and then Adrian came up with an idea:

"Well, we could tune down our instruments a step if needed."

"True, but didn't you once say that the Earth would complete a full rotation around the Sun and you'd still not be done with calibrating your floating bridge?" asked Steven.

"That's why I'll be using a pitch shifter pedal. Our school seems to provide us with all possible effects pedals for free here, so that's my problem solved. Callum and Jack don't have that issue."

"Well, so long as everyone's on board", said Steven.

"Yeah, all good on my end. I only have to tune my E string to a D", said Jack.

"Works for me as well", added Callum.

"Awesome. I'll keep working on these lyrics. If you have any ideas, just message them and I'll see if I can make it work."

As the most productive rehearsal session was coming to an end, the boys started packing their things up. On their way out, Parker asked Adrian:

"Hey, you said you had an old electric guitar you no longer use. Can I borrow it for a few days, along with an amp? I have had this riff idea in my head for a couple of days and I need the tools to bring it to life."

"Yeah, we can stop by our house and I'll give them to you, no problem."

"Cool. Any preferences on the beats or moods for these riffs by the way?"

"Not really. If a riff sounds good, regardless of the beat, we can make it work."

With that being said, everyone went home.

Parker's punk-rock riff

"Are you trying to push me out of the rhythm guitarist role?" a frustrated Callum asked.

"No, I just came up with a riff, just chill out for a bit", an annoyed Parker answered.

This conversation had been going on back and forth throughout the first 10 minutes of the boys' final rehearsal before Christmas break and Adrian, holding his head in his hands, finally decided to intervene:

"Alright, can the both of you please stop for a minute and tell me what's going on?"

"Well, remember how you lent me your old guitar so I could try out some riffs?"

"Yes, I do."

"Well, I finally came up with one that could work, but pinhead over here keeps saying I want to kick him off the rhythm guitar role."

"I see. Well, if you both recall, we did discuss back in like chapter five that you would become the drummer under the condition that we take a look at any music you write to see if it's a good fit. And pinhead over here was part of that discussion, so he should know better. Now, if both of you absolute melons would stop arguing for five minutes, maybe we could take a look at the riff that Parker wrote and see how it sounds."

Parker and Callum managed to shut up, while the others were silently observing the situation.

"How hard are you trying not to laugh right now, not-Rapunzel the lead singer?" Adrian asked his brother.

"They'll probably have to invent some new numbers to quantify that", not-Rapunzel the lead singer answered.

"I'm about to audibly sigh right now, just...show me the bloody riff."

After giving each other some mean looks and a couple of audible "hmphs", Parker and Callum got on stage and the former played the following riff:

```
              P.M.--|         P.M.--|         P.M.--|

        E | --------------------------------- |

        B | --------------------------------- |

        G | --------------------------------- |

        D | -3---------3---------3------ |

        A | -3---------3---------3------ |

        E | -1--1-1-1--1--1-1-1--1--1-1- |
```

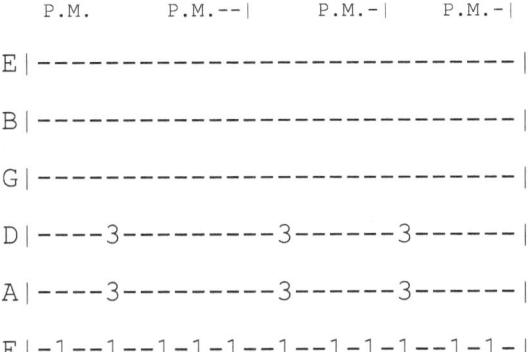

```
        P.M.         P.M.--|        P.M.-|       P.M.-|

    E |----------------------------------|

    B |----------------------------------|

    G |----------------------------------|

    D |----3---------3------3------|

    A |----3---------3------3------|

    E |-1--1--1-1-1--1--1-1-1--1-1-|
```

Author's note: two lines between notes means the note is an 8th note, one line between notes means the note is a 16th note; P.M. means palm mute.

"And basically, this pattern repeats itself. I haven't figured out too much with regards to the next steps but I enjoyed this particular riff."

"Yeah, no worries. It's quite the pacy riff that one, isn't it? It gives me some punk rock vibes", said Adrian.

"Sort of, I guess. I tried looking a bit into music theory and the difference between a major and minor scale and I have to say, I don't envision this one as a minor key song", added Parker.

"Hm, you might be on to something there."

The riff itself proved to be good enough to capture everyone's attention. Adrian picked up his guitar and started fiddling around with some power chords in the key of F major.

After a few minutes, he finally came up with the best continuation he thought would work, which was basically repeating the riff, but using the G5, Bb5, and A5 chords in separate bars, without any palm-muting.

"So, what do you all think?" he asked.

"Yep, that'll definitely do it", everyone agreed.

Parker also came up with some drum ideas for this riff and after a bit of a discussion, they decided that the riff itself should be played at first without the drums on the F5 chord, and then the drums would kick in and the whole section that Adrian came up with will be played.

The trouble was going forward after this section, as this worked well as an intro to the song:

"Doesn't it get quite boring if we keep the same pattern over and over during the verses?" asked Steven.

"It most definitely does, so I suggest this idea", said Jack, and then played the following part on his bass over and over on different notes:

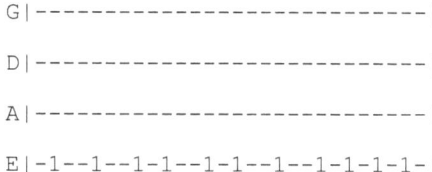

```
G|----------------------------|
D|----------------------------|
A|----------------------------|
E|-1--1--1-1--1-1--1--1-1-1-1-|
```

"That's actually a pretty cool continuation. We could do some palm-mutes on the 16th notes between the 8th notes there, on the guitar", added Parker.

"I suppose that's a good idea", muttered Callum to himself.

"What was that? Was it the muttered sound of approval?" asked Parker.

"Oh, it's an approval alright, the approval of me telling you to-"

"I'm going to take those drumsticks and make you sit on them throughout this whole rehearsal if you even dare start that feud again", an exasperated Adrian said.

Callum and Parker knew Adrian spoke very literally most of the time, so they decided to not take any chances on that.

The rest of the rehearsal went pretty smoothly. The boys even decided on a chorus, which would be Parker's initial riff, played on the C5, D5, F5, and D5 chords, with a bit of a transition between F5 and D5, and also between the D5 and the next phase:

```
E | ------------------------- |
B | ------------------------- |
G | -5--5-5-5--5--5-5-5--5--5-5- |
D | -5--5-5-5--5--5-5-5--5--5-5- |
A | -3--3-3-3--3--3-3-3--3--3-3- |
E | ------------------------- |
```

```
E|---------------------------|
B|---------------------------|
G|-5--5--5-5-5--5--5-5-5--5-5-|
D|-5--5--5-5-5--5--5-5-5--5-5-|
A|-3--3--3-3-3--3--3-3-3--3-3-|
E|---------------------------|


E|---------------------------|
B|---------------------------|
G|-7--7-7-7--7--7-7-7--7--7-7-|
D|-7--7-7-7--7--7-7-7--7--7-7-|
A|-5--5-5-5--5--5-5-5--5--5-5-|
E|---------------------------|


E|---------------------------|
B|---------------------------|
G|-7--7--7-7-7--7--7-7-7--7-7-|
D|-7--7--7-7-7--7--7-7-7--7-7-|
A|-5--5--5-5-5--5--5-5-5--5-5-|
E|---------------------------|


E|-------------------------------------|
B|-------------------------------------|
G|-10--10-10-10--10--10-10-10--10--10-10-|
D|-10--10-10-10--10--10-10-10--10--10-10-|
A|-8---8--8--8---8---8--8--8---8---8--8--|
E|-------------------------------------|
```

```
E|----------------------------------------|
B|----------------------------------------|
G|-10--10--10-10-10--10--10-9-10--10-9-|
D|-10--10--10-10-10--10--10-9-10--10-9-|
A|-8---8---8--8--8---8---8--7-8---8--7-|
E|----------------------------------------|
```

```
E|---------------------------|
B|---------------------------|
G|-7--7-7-7--7--7-7-7--7--7-7-|
D|-7--7-7-7--7--7-7-7-7--7-7-|
A|-5--5-5-5--5--5-5-5--5--5-5-|
E|---------------------------|
```

```
E|------------------------------|
B|------------------------------|
G|-7--7--7-7-7--10--10-10-9--9-9-|
D|-7--7--7-7-7--10--10-10-9--9-9-|
A|-5--5--5-5-5--5---8--8--7--7-7-|
E|------------------------------|
```

After this, there was going to be an interlude section, which was basically the intro riff with all the chords and no palm-muting. After that, the verses would be played again. Speaking of the verses, they were a combination of the two riffs that Jack and Parker came up with.

Jack's riff was used on the F5, G5, and A5 chords, while Parker's was used in the middle, on the Bb5 chord. There were going to be two verses and on the second one, on the A5 chord second measure, Adrian suggested they play it two times only, like two half notes basically, so it leads better into the chorus.

There was also going to be a solo, played over the verse riffs, and the interlude between the second chorus featured the drumming from the intro.

Steven then suggested that the final chorus should be played twice, to which everyone agreed. The final idea that was floating around was to have a fake intro, one that starts off a bit tamer, in order to surprise listeners when the main riff comes into play.

This idea was accepted with quite good energy by the others, and Adrian said he would come up with something. He already had the idea of using an acoustic guitar and some piano chords, that could also make a comeback during the outro of the song.

Theme-wise, they didn't have too many ideas about what to do with the song, and given that the holidays were coming up, they were just glad they had two good songs in progress.

As they were getting ready to go home, Avril, who had become their de facto spectator, came up to Steven and said:

"Hey, are you free later this afternoon? I want us both to go to this karaoke place so you can get accustomed to singing in public."

"*Yeah, that's the only reason you want to be alone with him...*" Adrian, who was in hearing range, thought to himself.

"I suppose I am", answered Steven.

"Excellent! Here's the location, we'll meet up there."

"That works. We are allowed to enter a karaoke bar, right?"

"This one is good, yes. There's a few of them dedicated to people under the legal drinking age, where no alcohol is served. It would have been weird to not have these places around given the whole high school competition."

"I see. Well, as my brother would put it, Millie's done his research."

"Who was this Millie again?" asked Avril.

"The guy who supposedly is writing this book which we are part of."

Avril squinted a bit in disbelief and then asked:

"How did Adrian not get lost at the shop as a child?"

"I moved my feet in the direction our mom told us to, until I was old enough to understand spatial awareness at an acceptable level", replied Adrian.

Avril was willing to accept this as an answer. With all this said and done, they all wished each other Happy Holidays, agreed to share any ideas and progress on the two songs they had, or any potential new ones, and also agreed to keep practicing.

Perhaps there was a bit of hope for this band after all.

Steven goes to karaoke

"I really don't know what to expect from karaoke", Steven noted.

"I know what you mean. It's going to be something of a new experience in and of itself, but having Avril as company surely doesn't help", said Adrian.

"I can hear that, you know", remarked Avril.

"I know. It was just my way of wondering why you're still here."

"We've been walking in the same direction after rehearsals for almost two months now, Adrian."

"Oh, right. I usually tune you out."

"Aww, are your systems broken? Do you need some sleep or some hot cocoa?" Avril asked mockingly.

"Ha-ha, you should be a comedian, it'd be some of the most riveting shows that no one will choose to see."

"I could go for some hot cocoa", said Steven, who was amused at his brother's back-and-forth with Avril.

"I think tea would be a better bet before singing", said Avril.

After having arrived at the point where their roads split, which was the bus station closest to Avril's home, two bus stops away from where the twins lived, Avril and Steven agreed to meet here instead of directly at the bar in two hours so they could go together.

The boys then went home and were greeted by the smell of freshly baked chestnuts, Christmas scones and traditional Christmas songs playing in the house. Given that it was a bit chilly outside, this sight made them feel quite relaxed.

After changing into something more comfortable, the twins sat down at the table and had a snack and some tea. They talked about their day with their parents and Steven informed them that he'd be going to the karaoke bar a bit later. His mother asked:

"That's nice to hear, dear. Are you going alone or with someone else?"

"Just me, though I'm fairly convinced there are going to be other people from other high schools. But that's about it."

"*Yeah, that's about it, and nothing else*", thought Adrian while being a bit amused. "*On the other hand, though, it gives me time to try and send out another complaint about Ryan, maybe fourth time's going to be the charm. Such a useless system, that.*"

He was referring to the complaint system their high school had implemented, where students could report if they were being harassed by other students and the acts would be dealt with accordingly. Adrian heard that most if not all students who used it had seen some improvements, but so far, nothing on his end.

After about an hour and a half, Steven started getting dressed, and was soon on his way to meet up with Avril. It was almost dark outside and it also started snowing, making it quite a peaceful walk. He was getting that weird feeling in his stomach again, but he assumed it was because he was nervous about singing.

He arrived just as Avril was arriving so they started walking towards the location. They were both a bit nervous and awkward, not knowing exactly what to say. It was the first time they were alone and outside of school, after all.

"So, what should I expect from karaoke afternoons or nights?" asked Steven after a while.

"Oh, they're usually quite fun. Given that we'll probably encounter some students from other high schools, or even our own, expect a couple of snide remarks as well." said Avril.

"That's about as reassuring as you telling me I'm not ready to meet your father. I'm curious though, what's he like?"

"Oh, he's uhm … quite protective. Like, he takes the dad talk thing way too seriously and it scares people a bit. Probably has something to do with his job."

"I see. I take it he scared a lot of potential boyfriends away?"

"Not really, because so far my luck with boys consists of this one guy I asked to be my date to the Freshman Ball, and who literally told me he found someone better during the event. No, my educated guess on the matter comes from our dinner talks, where he tells me that I should always look for someone who dresses well, makes me feel safe, isn't rude, bla-bla-bla."

"I see."

After a bit more walking in silence, Avril continued:

"What about you? Did you tell your parents where you're going?"

"Oh yes. I told them I'm going alone, which is sort of true because I left home alone and I happened to meet you on the way here, if someone asks. My parents would probably like you though."

"I mean, mine too, probably. I never really go into such talk with my folks, because I'd have to tell them about these two bandmates of mine who can't stop asking me out on dates. It's why I divide me time between Roxanne and you guys, it's been quite refreshing."

"I take it your bandmates are quite insistent in that regard?"

"Like you wouldn't believe. I tried being subtle, direct, and even ended up elbowing one of them in the stomach when he tried to hug me."

"Oh, I'm sorry to hear that."

"Yeah, it's not your fault, it's just...tiresome."

After a few more minutes, they finally arrived at their location and went in.

They were greeted by a symphony consisting of chatter, clinking bottles and glasses, and a somewhat decent performance of a pop song, which was in line with a place that went by the name of Pitch Perfect Pub.

While making their way to a table that Avril had reserved, Steven couldn't help but notice a couple of familiar faces from their high school, including three out of the five members of Monica's band, Adrian's former crush.

Having sat down, Avril laid out a plan for the afternoon:

"It seems a tad crowded, so I think we'll manage about three songs for today. I'm going to suggest some lower range, ballad-like songs for now. You have the range for more, but your mind doesn't know it yet, so it's best to start off with something more comfortable."

"That sounds good. Are you going to join me on stage?"

"Maybe for one of them, which is a duet of sorts, but other than that, you are going on your own. I'll put my songs right after yours as well."

As she was scanning the area, Avril noticed a couple of sarcastic and mocking looks from certain school mates and she wasn't about to let that slide. She went ahead and talked to the DJ and put their songs in. They had about three songs until Steven was up.

"Alright, all settled. Now I know you're a bit nervous, but you'll just have to trust that you know what you're doing. You have that song about being on the road, Turning Pages, the duet ballad I mentioned called The Space You Left, and a chill acoustic song about life called Letting Life Drift."

"I'm going to be fine, after all, I managed to shut up an entire courtyard full of students with two well placed remarks this one time." Steven then proceeded to tell Avril the story of when he drew the artists for Andrew F. Gordon High School.

The three songs seemed to fly by and there went Steven, up on the stage, to sing a song about being up on stage. The intro to Turning Pages is quite short, so there was little prep time. However, once he started singing, something changed in him, and it was a good thing.

Any and all nervousness had left his body and he was feeling like a true lead singer. Sure, his voice still had some places where it almost gave up and it was a bit weaker than what he wanted, but when he was in his comfort zone regarding the notes, they hit pretty hard for someone who had been practicing for about two months.

And his performance didn't go unnoticed, as he received quite his fair share of applause. When getting off the stage, he noticed that Avril was talking to another boy, someone who he did remember seeing once, though he couldn't pinpoint the exact place.

As she was getting ready to hit the stage, Steven was curious about that encounter. Avril just said, in a cryptic manner:

"Oh, you don't need to worry about him. I'll tell you more after my song, which is dedicated to him."

Steven was confused, but curious, so he went back at their table and waited. What followed was an incredibly powerful, punk, almost venomous interpretation of a break-up song called You Should Have Known.

Everyone in the public gave a thunderous round of applause to Avril and Steven finally remembered where he saw the boy from earlier. It was the person that Avril was arguing with at the Freshman Ball, and who dumped her in the middle of the event, as he previously learned.

"That was extremely good singing. I take it this was a dig at the one you talked to earlier?"

"Yeah, he wanted me to ditch you and hang out with him. It turns out his Freshman Ball fling sent him packing about 15 minutes after he left me there standing like a fool. I told him to come and talk to me after the song but I noticed he left shortly after the first chorus."

"I see. On the other hand, though, how many levels do I have to level up before I can sing like that?"

"Darling, I'm five years ahead of you in terms of vocals. However, you're nailing stuff faster than I was ever capable to so I'm thinking that this time, next year, you'll be able to do that and maybe even more, if we keep practicing."

Steven felt quite reassured by this statement. The next two songs proved to be quite fun as well. During The Space You Left, Avril did join him on stage and Steven noticed she got extremely emotional during the choruses. He decided not intrude, as he assumed it was something deeply personal. And during Letting Life Drift, he just had fun and managed to sing it correctly for the most part.

After Avril finished her other two songs, they put on their jackets and started walking home.

It had been snowing quite a bit while they were inside and this made for a very relaxing walk. For a while, the two of them walked in silence, but they did have a bit of a spring in their step. After a while, Avril asked:

"How did it feel on stage? It didn't seem like it was your first time, somehow you managed to look like a natural."

"I don't know, I just forget everything and have a good time. I apparently enjoy this a lot more than I had assumed I would. It's fun. You also did wonders on that stage, it was awesome."

"Thanks. I have a lot of stuff that needs to come out of me when I'm up there. Mostly frustration, angst, and...other things", added Avril with a bit of hesitation.

"Well, just make sure you don't run out of that angst before the competition is over", said Steven, opting to ignore her hesitation.

"Have you met my band members? They spend half of their time trying to convince me to go out on a date with them, and the other half clunking their way to half-decent performances. Honestly, if I had another possibility, I'd go in another band, but no one really tolerates me outside of you, your brother, my best friend and classmate Roxanne, and those three jesters.

On the plus side, it seems one of them is slowly backing out, so at least it's more manageable."

"I assume it's the one who you personally introduced to your elbow. How do they tolerate you spending so much time with me?"

"Oh, they hate you, you are public enemy number one to them. It's funny hearing them scheme and talk bad about you, they sound like two or three mildly mannered conniving cartoon characters, it's quite the sight."

"I'm more surprised they haven't like challenged me to a duel or something."

"Funnily enough, this is exactly what they're planning, but they want to do it in phases. The first one would be challenging your brother to a guitar duel. Their bright idea is to mock him before rehearsal to see his reaction and what he can play."

Steven chuckled and said:

"If you want them to back off, this is exactly what you should encourage them to do. Unlike me, Adrian is merciless when it comes to such things. And he might not have shown that yet, but he has the skills to back it up. The level you're at with singing is the level he's at with guitar, on an off day nonetheless."

"You know what? You made me curious. I think I'll tell them to do just that after we get back from holiday."

As the two of them hatched up this somewhat nefarious scheme, they arrived at Avril's bus station.

"Well, I guess this is where our karaoke night ends. It's been quite a nice experience, I'm glad you had me along for the ride", said Steven, awkwardly moving his right foot through the snow, switching between glancing at Avril and at other elements between them.

"Yeah, I ... I enjoyed it too", she answered in a delicate manner.

"I guess I'll be going home now. Happy Holidays and I guess I'll see you in January."

"Sounds about right. Happy Holidays to you too!" said Avril, waving her hand.

Steven turned around and started walking. Avril then called him:

"Hey, wait up a bit, please."

Steven stopped, turned around again, and was met with a great big hug from Avril, who was running towards him. He returned the gesture, thinking to himself:

"*You know what, hugs* are *nice.*"

"Thanks for being there for me and for sticking by me after that first day encounter", added Avril and let go.

Steven nodded as a way of saying "No worries", and they waved each other good bye and went home. He walked for a bit until he knew she was out of sight, then stopped to appreciate what had happened. It was one of those moments he wanted to last forever, though he was still unaware of why that was the case. Feeling very happy and giddy inside, he had quite the spring in his step going home.

He arrived just in time for supper. The warm feeling from inside the house made him relax even more, considering that it became really chilly outside and it had been snowing even more.

The four members of the Milner family then enjoyed a lovely and relaxing dinner. Steven told them all about how he felt on stage and how he enjoyed himself.

After a very delicious dessert, the boys went to their rooms as the parents decided to watch some television. Adrian decided to poke his brother for more teenage-appropriate information:

"You seem very happy, but it's a different kind of happiness. What happened out there?"

"Nothing special, just had a good time and felt really good on stage. It's post-concert enthusiasm, if you will."

"Uh-huh. No, that's not it. You winning matches on consoles is nothing special, this is different. And I've seen you being happy after nailing songs, and it's not that either. So, what is it?"

Steven hesitated for a bit. But he decided to continue:

"Listen, I'll tell you, but you can't tell Mom or Dad. Just before we went home, she hugged me and thanked me for being there for her and giving her a second chance. And it felt really, really good. It felt like one of those moments you'll always remember...how do you call them?"

"Core memories?"

"Yeah, that. I just can't stop thinking about it. Why do you think that is?"

Adrian squinted a bit while looking at his brother, smiled, and then answered:

"Yow two are the most precious people I know. And I'd tell you what's going on but I'd rather let the both of you figure it out."

"I don't get it."

"Oh, you will. Just give it time."

The boys then went and took a shower, had some fun on their console and went to bed.

Holiday time

Christmas time was finally here and the twins were very happy. It was a time of relaxation that both Steven and Adrian were looking forward to. Between the free time and Christmas-themed activities, there was a lot to choose from in terms of things to do.

Presents wise, Steven got a new orange shirt he'd been wanting for a while and Adrian got some new strings for his guitar which, to his shame, was long overdue a change in that area.

Adrian was noticeably happier than in previous years during this time and it was due to them having two songs to work with for their album. His ideal schedule would have them finish writing and maybe recording at least five songs until the end of ninth grade, which seemed a bit impossible a few weeks ago, but was now definitely within reach.

And it also helped that the other members of their band had also become a tad more creative. Callum managed to come up with a new pop-punk riff which Adrian was instantly hooked on, while Parker managed to come up with some intro drums, while also having an idea on how to continue with a double-kick pattern, which was a good thing, since it's very characteristic of heavy metal songs.

And to top it all off, during Christmas Eve, Steven picked up his acoustic guitar, tuned it to drop D, yelled "Hey Adrian, look, drop D tuning" and somehow managed to come up with a perfect drop D idea that could work as a heavy metal song. His brother tweaked it a bit into a working riff and even came up with a variation of it so they would have two different riffs playing during the verses. And after that, he recorded a rough demo of it and sent it over to the others to see if any drums and bass ideas would come up.

Steven also continued his vocal practice, becoming ever so close to adding rasp to his singing. He wasn't quite there yet, and Avril always mentioned that if he felt anything hurting in his throat, he would need to stop right then and there.

A few houses away, Avril was also enjoying quite a lovely Christmas. After the karaoke afternoon with Steven, she went home feeling really good and happy. Her mother noticed the change in her demeanor and tried to find out why that was. Avril successfully convinced her that it was because she performed well on stage. Her mother knew it was bound to be more than that, but decided to play along. And she wasn't wrong, because Avril was also thrilled when she got a Merry Christmas message from Steven.

The fact that it snowed a fair bit also contributed to the storybook feeling of the holidays, from Christmas all the way to New Year's Eve and the first few days of the new year. Everyone felt rested, their energy levels were at a good level, and while going back to school isn't something that anyone enjoys that much, the twins were ready to go again.

Guitar duels and Avril's desolate past

January seemed to breeze by in a flash, to everyone's joy because it had proven to be quite a cold and grey month. Steven and the boys were well on their way to perfecting three songs. The songs themselves had the tentative titles Graduation, Adrenaline Rush, and A Slight Amount Of Anger, with the last one being based on Steven's drop D riff. Callum's second pop-punk riff was also in line to become a song soon.

Jack noted that Adrian was seemingly quiet in the songwriting department. His response was a mysterious one, implying that he was actually working on at least two songs, but wanted to show them off when they were more complete. Steven confirmed that his brother did indeed have some files on their computer which pointed to that being true.

In the meantime, Avril had been busy with a bit of mischief. And that mischief had something to do with getting her guitarist bandmate Dan to challenge Adrian to a duel. And it seems that the first rehearsal of February was the one when she chose to put this plan into action.

After having finished their last song, Avril and the others made way for Steven and Adrian's band to walk on stage. She also gave a sort of a head nod towards her guitarist, Dan, pointing the finger towards Adrian at the same time. And Dan knew what he had to do.

"Hello there, Milner. In case you don't know me, I am-"

"Dan, masquerade guitarist, made to look way better than you should by a competent lead singer and rhythm guitarist", answered Adrian, who was busy hooking up his guitar to his amp and didn't even bother to look at Dan while answering. Noticing the awkward silence and turning around to see a flabbergasted look on him, he continued:

"Oh, I'm sorry, you wanted to make yourself cool and I interrupted you."

"Oh, a wise guy, eh?"

"That insult only works if I wasn't in fact wiser than you."

"Those snide remarks are going to get you in trouble someday."

"No, these snide remarks are me being as calm as possible towards someone who's looking for a fight. Also, I carried weight that was way harder than how hard you think your lines are hitting right now, so what is it that you want?"

Avril, Steven and the others couldn't help but snicker at this banter. Noticing this, Dan tried to regain his composure, but his body language wasn't helping him look all that convincing, unlike Adrian, who was now standing up and was extremely confident in his stance.

"I'm here to challenge you to a duel", Dan finally muttered.

"You know that usually ends up badly for someone, right?"

"Not that kind of duel, dummy, a guitar duel."

"Oh, that's an even worse idea for you, like, the most horrible idea possible. Seriously, who hates you this much? What could you have possibly done to deserve such an outcome?"

"Listen, I know you like to boast and talk a great talk and all that but-"

"I'm not boasting, Dan. I have about two minutes until our rehearsal begins and I'm trying my best to get you out of here with some semblance of reputation intact. I've seen your skills my man, I've seen how tense you are during the solos you're supposed to be playing. You're very obviously skipping notes on difficult ones to adapt them to your abilities. This will end very badly for you."

Dan wasn't budging, so on the surface, Adrian had no other option but to accept this challenge.

"Avril my dear, this one is for you", shouted Dan.

Finally understanding what this was about, Adrian's facial expression changed from sarcastic to locked in, almost evil. Steven and Avril were still completely clueless about their feelings, but Adrian could see them from a mile away, and he was not about to let someone like Dan try to ruin it. He then turned to him:

"You first, Dan...", he said, with one of the most hair-raising tones that anyone in the room had ever heard.

Dan was terrified after hearing that voice and could barely muster any strength in his hands. He managed to play a somewhat decent, almost shredding passage in the A minor pentatonic scale. Upon finishing it, he said to Adrian, in a somewhat trembling voice, trying to sound confident:

"Your turn now."

Avril and Steven had noticed the change in Adrian's demeanor, tone, and behavior and were brimming with enthusiasm and some slight anxiety at what was about to come.

Adrian asked them both, in an even more frightening tone:

"You two, is it safe to assume I tried everything in my power to prevent what is about to happen?"

After seeing them both nod in agreement, he looked Dan dead in the eyes before flawlessly playing the tapping intro from one of the songs they rehearsed a lot, an incredibly difficult solo from one of the tie-breaker songs, a shredding passage from what was the solo he was working on for Adrenaline Rush, and ended with a solo labelled as impossible to play live by the original creator, since he never assumed he'd have to do it.

The stunned silence that followed from everyone was deafening. Adrian slowly put his guitar into a stand on the stage, slowly walked towards Dan, and said:

"We're done here. Now, get off the stage, let us rehearse in peace, and please, oh please, tell your friends about me. And don't say I didn't warn you."

For the first time today, Dan was speechless and decided to take Adrian's suggestion and walked off stage, barely able to look at anyone.

Once that was done, Adrian calmly informed his bandmates:

"We can start now, please. Let's do a bit of warm-up and then try and work on the three songs we have. Steven finally finished the lyrics for Graduation and I think I finally have a theme idea for Adrenaline Rush and a solo for it, part of which you've already heard."

"You think that guy's going to be alright?" asked Steven, still recovering from earlier.

"Yes, he just took a great blow to his ego. His body language is telling me he is merely questioning his existence. This guy is basically Ryan if he were a guitarist. And I'm fairly confident I'm not the only one who can notice this", said Adrian, subtly looking towards Avril.

"I see. By the way, what's the status on Ryan?" asked Parker.

"Five complaint forms in, no results. Basically, what I was expecting, though not what I was hoping for. You're not secretly deleting those things from the high school database, right?" Adrian asked Parker.

Parker shook his head in strong disagreement and got on the drums.

One of the unexpected side effects of the earlier duel was that everyone else finally got to see Adrian's ability in action. So far, he had been quite shy in showing off what he was capable of as a lead guitarist, leading to Parker even questioning if he wants the band to succeed. But any and all doubts of such nature were now completely gone.

The rehearsal went extremely well, and Steven was even getting a bit of a grip with adding rasp to his vocals, though he still couldn't quite control it correctly. Turns out relying on vocal fry had the desired effect, when done right.

After the rehearsal was over, everyone started walking home. Adrian, Steven and Avril were walking as per usual, but the former noticed that the latter was dragging her steps a bit.

"Look, I'm sorry I went so hard on Dan. He'll be fine, it may actually help him focus on becoming a better guitarist."

"Oh, it's not that, I was hoping for exactly that when I coerced him into this duel. It's something else entirely. Do you have 10 minutes to spare for today?" Avril asked, her voice becoming frail.

Noticing the shift in tone, Adrian became serious and without hesitation, said:

"Yes. I know a place in this lovely courtyard where no one will bother us."

They went in one of the grassy areas from the courtyard, quite a bit away from the main high school building. Avril noticed that this place allowed you to keep an eye on what was going on in most of the courtyard, without having the risk of someone surprising you from behind. In her head, she likened this to how cats like to stand on the edge of the bed for somewhat similar reasons and the possibility of a quick escape.

The ground was a bit too cold to sit on, but luckily, they had some benches there that were free. Once the trio had sat down, Avril took a couple of deep breaths and started telling a story she had told only three other people before: her parents and Roxanne.

"It was a regular summer day. I was on my way to my friend Debbie's house like I had promised the other day. Just as I left, she sent me this cryptic text thanking me for being her friend and for always being there for her. I didn't take too much notice of it at the time, but I did speed up a bit, as something felt off."

Avril paused for a bit, took a few more deep breaths, and continued:

"There was a bit of a pile-up accident on my way there and quite a few people had blocked the pavement, making it difficult to walk. I managed to push my way through and started running. When I arrived, I was greeted by her mother. She told me Debbie was in her room, so I took my shoes off and ran up. Her mother noticed my jittery and alert tone, and went to turn off the stove as she was baking something. When I got up to her room I...I..."

Avril's voice was trembling and she started sobbing a quite a bit. Through the sobs she managed to continue:

"I stood there, in her doorway, like an idiot, not knowing what to do. I wanted to scream, but the words wouldn't come out, I want to run towards her, but my feet wouldn't move. When her mother came up and saw what had happened, she immediately called an ambulance, but it was too late."

Avril paused again, and after a few more sobs, she added:

"I've spent the last two and a half years wondering if I could have done something differently, what I missed, how I could have prevented it, if I could have saved her if I hadn't lost five minutes due to people staring at the world's most boring accident where three cars gently tapped each other and the result were three barely visible bumps."

Wiping some more tears away, Avril concluded:

"It took me this long to finally be able to read the autopsy results. She was gone five minutes after she sent me the text. It's the weirdest way to get closure for some of the things, but it's better than nothing. In her final note, she apologized for not being able to go on, and she hoped I'd find some people that will help me move on. And I don't know what stars or constellations made that possible, but I thank them for doing it."

Steven and Adrian were very touched by the final remark. The trio stood in silence for a few seconds. Steven then said:

"I'm sorry for your loss. I'm not going to attempt to say I understand how you feel. But we're here for you."

"Yes, we are", added Adrian in an uncharacteristically low and emotional voice. "Also, apologies again for almost pushing these buttons during our first day encounter."

"Thank you", said Avril. "And again, don't worry about the first day, I'll always appreciate you stopping and respecting my privacy when I asked you to. I just wanted to get this off my chest as well because...well, because I finally managed to confront one of the bigger inner demons I was fighting. I'm never going to forget Debbie and I do check on her mother from time to time. She is also in a better place mentally. She's the one that showed me the autopsy results."

After a few more minutes of silence, she continued:

"This bracelet on my hand is one we made together in class when we were in elementary school. She wanted to go all purple and pink, which are two words that were not and are still not really in my vernacular, so we compromised and made two: one in her style, and one a little more goth and gloomy for me. I never took it off my hand since we made it."

The tension was very much lifted as Avril stopped crying and was feeling a lot better:

"Our first day encounter is also why I knew I could trust you to put an end to Dan's obnoxious behavior towards me without sending him down a dangerous path. We seem to be fans of similar books regarding human behavior so I was certain you are going to know if and when you need to stop."

"Dan's the type of guy who would start spreading rumors about people he dislikes. At least now, he'll start spreading the truth and also keep away from you and Steven...and your vocal lessons with him", added Adrian at the end, not wanting to say something awkward.

"It's going to be quite refreshing, that. I think I'm ready to go home now", she added.

The three of them started walking towards the exit. Avril was feeling genuinely happy inside, Adrian was thankful his mouth didn't get the better of him a few months back, and Steven finally understood why Avril's voice was quivering when singing The Space You Left. He also couldn't help but admire the guts she had for agreeing to sing that on stage with him.

"Hey, do you feel like joining us at The Multiverse Junction? It's a local comic book store where we hang out from time to time."

"Yeah, I think I have the time. I'm not into comics that much, but my dad is, so I know a fair bit about them. I'm fairly confident he took a lot of inspiration from those stories whenever he told me bedtime stories when I was little", Avril chuckled.

"Sounds about right. Be warned though, given that you're a girl, you're a bit of a rare sight with some of the customers there. They're not Dans or anything like that, but they will be in awe of your presence. And they'll attempt to talk to you, but will somehow sound even clunkier than the guy who invited a girl to the Freshman Ball, only to be told they'll meet there, just so he can see who her actual date was", added Adrian.

"Beats having an accepted invitation and getting dumped there for someone else", said Avril.

Adrian looked at Avril with a bit of disbelief, but he wasn't able to detect any hint of sarcasm on her face, which meant that she was most likely telling the truth.

"Yeah, I can't argue with that, you had it worse there", he said.

They went to the comic book store, where Avril learned about the arrangements between the twins and Dennis and was quickly added the list of people allowed at their chosen table. After that, they started scanning through the available issues and bought some refreshments.

The expelled students mystery

Finding out about Avril's past tragedy had brought the trio closer together, though Adrian would be hard pressed to admit he enjoyed the girl's company. However, he did enjoy seeing his brother and Avril get closer and bringing out the best in each other.

Music wise, it was also going great. They had finally put together the pieces for the three songs they had in progress and they had also learned that they could record them at their high school.

As it turns out, each and every band had access to a personal laptop especially optimized for music production. And when they finally got access to it, you could actually see Adrian's eyes light up with joy, as it came prepared with fully licensed virtual instruments ranging from drums and strings to the most versatile amp sims known to musicians. And of course, any and all EQs, delays, and other tools required for mixing and mastering were readily available.

Adrian decided he'd be the one in charge of mixing and mastering, and since no one really wanted to go through the ropes of learning everything in as much detail as he already knew, they all agreed. Steven was glad this was the case as he could work alongside him and maybe pick up some new tricks.

Recording guitars, bass, and voice was no issue, but trying to record drums proved to be quite the challenge and for now, the boys decided to go with programmed MIDI drums, since the rules clearly stated that there would be no points deducted or added if some bands decided to use such drums instead of real ones. Luckily for Parker, an electronic drumkit was also made available at their high school, so he hooked it up to the laptop and recorded the MIDI parts.

As such, the next two months were spent recording and producing the three songs they had finished. Adrian hoped to finish everything before Easter break, which proved to be a challenge due to the amount of other school work he had to do but also due to an interesting thing he learned from Avril along the way.

One time, as the boys were getting ready for their rehearsal and still putting off the quest to finding a name for their band, Avril got off stage after her rehearsal, but instead of finding a seat, she packed her stuff and was about to leave.

"Hey, how come you're not staying this time around?" asked Steven.

"Well, I got into a bit of mischief and headmaster Turner wants to see me. Did you know it was frowned upon to mock your teacher's gestures behind their back?"

"Uhm...yes?"

"Yeah, it's fairly obvious in hindsight, now that I think about it. The teacher in question was very angrily saying this. But then again, I kept doing it for the last six months and no one batted an eye. This time around, someone snitched on me."

"Any idea who?"

"Probably Dan as retaliation for the complete and utter humiliation I put him through. He still hasn't quit the band but him and Van have both stopped trying to ask me out for the time being."

"And here I was thinking you realized our music is too good and were about to go tell your band to quit and just support us instead. Mischief fits you better though", said Adrian as he was readying his guitar and helping Callum and Jack with theirs.

"Uhm...thanks, I guess. Don't you worry your boring little grey t-shirt though, I'll be back after the meeting to tell you all about it."

So, the boys got to recording their parts for the song Graduation while Avril went to headmaster John Turner's office. She was welcomed by his assistant, a lovely woman in her 40s, who asked her to wait outside the office for a bit as the headmaster was currently in a meeting with someone.

As she was waiting, she noticed that on the wall outside the headmaster's office, there were pictures with every generation of students from this high school, which was quite a tall ask, given the long history. The pictures had two columns each, the one on the left showing the students as freshmen and the one on the right showing them as graduates.

Since she had a bit of time as the meeting was extended a bit, Avril started analyzing each and every picture. They all looked pretty much the same but she did notice something odd. During the last thirty years or so, every few generations, there seemed to be one or two students missing from the column on the right. Her first thought was to think that something tragic must have happened, but she shrugged it off.

"Hm, this is odd. Whatever happened to you people? Moving high schools is not something that happens that often given the size of this city. And it's especially odd that this only started happening in the last thirty years. Lucky for me, I know who to ask for more details and I especially know who to ask to help me dig up whatever I can't find out today", Avril thought to herself.

"Miss Lawson? The headmaster will see you now", the assistant told Avril.

"Wonderful, can't wait", she muttered under her breath as she went into his office.

Avril was quite impressed by the order she saw in every cabinet, which was visible given that the doors had windows on them. The office itself was quite well lit, even having a window to the outside, allowing for a lot of natural light to come in and show off the wonderful craftsmanship of the brown cabinets, that looked like they had been there since the high school was built. They were very well maintained and extremely clean.

The headmaster's desk was the only place where order couldn't find a place, as the inordinate amount of file stacks were barely allowing anyone to see the headmaster's face and chair whenever he was talking.

Avril sat down in front of the headmaster's desk, and waited for him to finish typing something on his keyboard. John Turner was a very elegant person, his deep blue suit, white shirt and black tie perfectly complimenting his grey hair. Avril thought he looked like a spy novel character, though she was hoping he was more on the hero's side rather than the villainous one.

"Welcome, Ms. Lawson", the headmaster spoke, with a gentle, baritone-like voice. "I see you've gotten yourself into a bit of trouble. Were you not aware that mocking your teachers is something they do not take kindly to?"

"Only if said teachers are stuck up little...I mean, I was probably made aware once upon a time, but I forgot. But come on, is it really worth wasting your time on this? I mean what if...what if I am allergic to bees and I saw one and was waving my hands trying to make it go away?"

"Ms. Lawson, I've been headmaster of this lovely institution for almost three decades now. I've seen many mischievous students, heard quite a lot of creative excuses, some believable, and some downright droll, and I am sorry to disappoint you, but that is not even the most creative excuse I've heard today, let alone this week. So, why don't we try this again?"

"Well, you see, it's...wait, did you say three decades?"

"I did. Why do you ask?"

"Well, I was planning on coming up with something better than the feather-brained thing I said earlier, but I got terribly distracted by the pictures of generations past outside your office. And I was wondering what correlation is it between your time here as headmaster and the seemingly unexplainable increase of students not finishing four years of high school here. While, of course, making sure I don't become one of them", said Avril, trying but failing to force an innocent smile.

"I shall answer your question in more detail after we discuss your behavioral conundrum. But rest assured, what those students did is far more dreadful than what you have done."

"Oh, good, then the line is further than what I did, good to know", muttered Avril.

"Ms. Lawson..."

"Alright, fine, I am sorry for mocking my teacher's hand gestures", said Avril, with a bit of an eye roll. "But do you have any idea how boring English literature becomes when we're trying to figure out what some long-ago dead people are trying to say?"

"So basically, what you're doing when studying the lyrics written by singers and musicians long since passed?"

"Well, yes, but the songs I listen to are cool, not boring."

"Ms. Lawson, I can tell you're not a malicious person, because otherwise, this conversation would have turned a different corner right now. With that being said, this is not a detention worthy gesture, but I would like to inform you that should it happen again, I will put you in detention."

"Good. Now, about those students..."

"I wasn't finished. I am going to require you to come by my office tomorrow and help arrange these files and put them in cabinets. I don't particularly trust technology all that much for certain things. I will give you a detailed list of the contents of each cabinet and you can sort of file here in the right one. Any questions?"

"Can I get expelled for a day instead?"

"No, you may not."

"Oh. Alright, at least I tried. Now, about those students..."

"Very well, Ms. Lawson, I shall attempt to be succinct, as I am sure you're looking forward to going back to the Milner twins' rehearsal."

"Yes, well...I...vocal...lessons for Steven...you know, teacher of voice, uhm, things", babbled Avril.

"Ms. Lawson, might I suggest using letters to form syllables, that you can in turn use to form words, that in turn form sentences and in the end, phrases? I would assume you wanted to say something along the lines of you being Steven's vocal teacher and are helping him learn new abilities."

Avril decided to just nod in agreement this time.

"Magnificent. Regarding those students, all of them ended up expelled due to various instances of egregious misbehavior. Not mocking teachers or talking back to them mind you, but seemingly normal students that have had photographic or video evidence of them assaulting other students. When confronted, the attackers of course all claimed innocence but the victims had bruises that matched the video or photographic evidence of places they were seemingly hit. As such, I had not alternative than to expel them. They did however manage to finish high school in one of the neighboring towns."

"Curious thing..." noted Avril.

"Quite so. Their names are not erased from our archives or history but let's just say they are not remembered as fondly as others."

"Did you or someone else investigate further to see what was causing these sudden changes in behavior?"

"Ms. Lawson, I am far too busy to include such activities in my daily tasks. And I know not of any other teachers that were of the curious sorts regarding these ordeals."

"Why am I not surprised. Anyhow, would that be all? Can I be excused now?"

"You may. See you tomorrow after school, Ms. Lawson. Do not be late."

Avril left the headmaster's office and went back to the rehearsal room, where recording was in progress, sort of. Things went quite well for the first hour, but then Callum and Parker started bickering a bit about the drum parts, and despite Adrian's best efforts, they were still not seeing eye-to-eye or ear-to-ear yet.

Taking advantage of this short break, Avril managed to sneak back into the room and soon arrived next to Steven and Adrian. Steven welcomed her back with open arms and the two of them hugged for quite a bit.

"So, how was it?" Steven asked.

"Boring, annoying, and predictable. I have to help him put some files in order or something. But the more interesting thing is I think I have found a mystery worth investigating, if you're up to it."

"I am, though I will want Adrian to tag along as well, this is more up his alley rather than mine."

"Yeah, it's alright. I'm assuming it will help to have him invested in something other than his guitar."

"Like that's ever going to happen", said Adrian, who was in ear-shot of this conversation. "So, what's this mystery about?"

Avril then proceeded to tell the twins what she had learned from headmaster Turner and Adrian agreed that something felt off. Monodia was known for its musicians and how sometimes their ego would get the best of them in interviews and whatnot, but outright fights or assaults were basically unheard of.

The trio agreed to have some fun with this information and to start digging around to see if they could find anything remotely interesting.

Adrian then went to put a stop to all the bickering so they could get some decent drum takes. It took a bit of convincing, but Parker was finally able to make amends with Callum once again and record his drums, which turned out to be quite good.

Afterwards, Adrian saved the project and packed the laptop so he could start working on the mixing and mastering aspects of the song, alongside Steven. Once he had a working version, he'd share it with everyone so they could all agree on a working mix.

Confrontation time

Summer break was just around the corner and between songwriting, end of the year tests, music production, and investigative activities, the gang's brains were a bit overheating to say the least.

Having finished recording, mixing, and mastering three songs already, they started working on the fourth one, which was based on Callum's second pop-punk riff, and on a fifth one, which was a more complex one put together by Adrian.

The latter got the idea by combining the cheerful aspects of pop-punk songs and the longer, more complex varieties of heavy metal songs, into one song. Basically, he was trying to accomplish writing a major scale song that combines aspects from both genres.

One of the more challenging tests from this final stretch of their school year was the mathematics test, for which everyone had been studying quite a bit. Professor Stevens was a kind teacher in many aspects, but when it came to mathematics, she was always expecting the best from her students, and this time around it was no different. Adrian knew this and he took things very seriously.

The test proved to be a very challenging one and once it was finished, the twins started discussing it in great detail:

"So, how did you find that abomination of a test to be?" asked Steven who was visibly tired after it.

"You know how these things go. I am fairly certain 75 percent of it is correct, and what I could not do, I faked it a bit until I got something that seemed right and fulfilled the requirements."

"I see. From what you told me, statistics say that you are as close as possible to a math God if you get six out of the ten exercises correctly. So, in keeping with your weird references, I'm guessing the next step for you is to dye your hair pink and become a maniacal version of yourself."

Adrian though about entertaining this idea, but decided he had more important things to focus on.

"Nah, I have more pressing matters. I've dug seeking treasure items regarding the expelled students and found very little, but I know there's more to it than what we know so far. The maniacal upgrade is going to have to wait."

The mathematics class was the last one of the school day so the twins started packing up and got ready to go home. On their way out of the classroom, they happened upon Ryan, who was in no rush to get out of the way.

"Oh, sorry, there's been a new directive coming from our headmaster. He says that geeks are to stay behind and clean up the classroom."

Steven was rolling his eyes at what he considered one of the most pathetic attempts at a joke he ever heard and went around Ryan, who failed to stop him. Adrian however, had other plans, considering that now six complaint tickets regarding his classmate's behavior had done nothing:

"Tell me something Ryan, did your parents try to have their own I-want-a-superhero-child moment and smacked you over the head one too many times while you were growing up?" asked Adrian while taking a somewhat attacking stance that made Ryan back up a few steps.

"Whoa, someone is up for a fight everyone!" shouted Ryan, trying to keep his cool.

"Far from it. For someone intent on making me cry, you sure do backpedal a lot. You'd be national champion at that if it was a sport. On that note, why are you so determined to see other teenage boys cry? Is it some weird turn-on you're trying to popularize or what?"

"You'd better watch your mouth, Milner."

"You'd better watch your step, else you might trip and fall over, which would only be the fifth most humiliating moment you've ever had to deal with during this year. The other four of course are the four rejections you got from the girls in our class. Basically, half of the girls from this classroom want nothing to do with you. You're somehow doing worse than me, at least I can get some sort of sympathy looks from people because I have to endure your pitiful attempts at mockery."

Ryan was trembling and he started to clench his jaw, a gesture that did not go unnoticed by Adrian.

"Little jaw movement there, eh, Ryan? Well, come on, show the world your strength, Ryan Harrisson. After all, with how much you've spent telling everyone you're basically the super human of Monodia, some wise guy with hearing protection should pose no threat or challenge to you."

Ryan wanted to attack, quite badly, but something was holding him back. Maybe it was fear, or maybe it was the fact that Adrian was so confident in his stance and his words. One thing was for sure, though, he was unable to do anything.

Noticing the commotion, other classmates started to join in. Ryan was hoping for some form of support, but he got very little encouragement for his behavior. Adrian was not necessarily the most popular kid in class, but given that he was genuinely a calm, collected person, that wasn't looking for any validation, he was usually on people's good side, unlike his current battle counterpart.

"People can't seem to grasp the fact that I talk literally, but if you just turn around and walk away, I'll legitimately stop trying to send in useless complaints to the headmaster. It would mean that there is some form of grey matter inside that skull of yours and the system is useless."

Considering the conversation over, Adrian went around Ryan and towards his brother and Avril, who were anxiously waiting for him. However, his gut was telling him that this was not over and he kept looking straight towards Steven and Avril's faces, since they could see behind him.

Ryan was absolutely fuming and livid after this encounter. Some of the other classmates were trying to calm him down, but it was too late, he started seeing red and bolted towards Adrian. He had his eyes set on his protective headphones.

Noticing the change in Steven's demeanor and him frantically pointing behind him, Adrian knew what was about to happen, so he took a defensive stance and turned around just in time to grab Ryan's hand, and slightly twist it to the right, enough to stop his movement and for it to hurt.

Professor Stevens, who was quickly summoned by Steven when he saw his brother confront Ryan, arrived just as Adrian stopped Ryan's hand.

"What is going on here?" she asked with a firm tone.

"I like to call this exhibit A of what happens when bullies don't get their comeuppance from professors", answered Adrian, now using both hands to try and restrain Ryan.

"Mr. Harrisson, cease your behavior immediately", said professor Stevens in a very adamant tone.

Realizing there was nothing left for him to do, Ryan conceded he had lost and stopped trying to take Adrian's headphones out. The latter then proceeded to take something out of his backpack:

"Here you are professor, in case he tries to claim his innocence", he said, handing physical copies of all the complaints that were sent regarding Ryan's behavior.

Going through them, professor Stevens was absolutely livid with disgust:

"Mr. Harrisson, if your parents are not present tomorrow to discuss this appalling behavior, you shall be expelled in due course. I suggest you take this warning seriously, as I am not in the mood for jokes."

Ryan was now completely terrified and barely managed to mutter:

"Yes, professor..."

"Mr. Milner, I do believe these would be of better use if I pass them along to headmaster Turner."

"Where do you think I am going next, professor? Keep them, I made more than enough copies."

Adrian then started walking towards the headmaster's office, along with Steven and Avril, who were intent on going in as witnesses.

An even more intriguing mystery

Adrian's classmates were still recovering from the earlier encounter. Most of them were on Adrian's side, with the very few people trying to support Ryan getting such cold views that they decided to just shut up.

As for Ryan, he was feeling humiliated, and terrified that his parents are now going to find out about his antics. It also didn't help that his eyes met those of Jordan, the girl he had the biggest crush on, who just looked at him while shaking her head in disgust.

In the meantime, the trio were walking towards headmaster Turner's office at a rapid pace.

"So, I was just wondering, how come you didn't try to intervene in any way?" a curious Avril asked Steven.

"We have a strict no-violence-unless-put-in-an-android-vs-teenager type scenario, name still in progress, Adrian's conception based on this animated show from the outside world."

"Indeed, we do. Steven usually just ignores such people, while my way of handling this is to take a few minutes to figure out potential weak points, all the while deflecting with some odd musical references. It's when I completely drop those jokes that one should know I am angry. I also know a fair few defensive tricks thanks to some martial arts lessons from a friend of Dad's, who's a sensei."

"I see. Well, with this Ryan character, you've had a few months of analysis in certain regards", added Avril.

"There was very little to analyze. He tries desperately to portray himself as this alpha male, while being completely and utterly oblivious to the fact that very few girls from our class actually like him or his attitude. Or guys for that matter."

"Yeah, I could tell that most of the class was either neutral or on your side there."

"People generally try to stay on my good side mostly due to the fact that I also try and stay neutral to all of them. Helping them out with any homework questions they have also helps."

Having arrived at the headmaster's office, they were greeted by his assistant:

"Sorry, you can't go in right now", she said.

"I do believe doors were invented for this exact purpose. Luckily for us, they were also equipped with this wonderful mechanism that allows us to go beyond them", said Adrian, while opening the door that led to the directorial office area.

"No, I mean the headmaster is currently in a meeting."

"Well, he is going to learn the definition of multitasking then", added Adrian, who was all but done with pleasantries at this point.

Avril and Steven were a bit surprised by his very unswerving answers and attitude, with Avril even asking Steven:

"Did you put something in his cocoa puffs this morning or what?"

"He doesn't eat cocoa puffs."

"Oh."

"Yeah, he used to love them, but then one day, he decided he doesn't want to eat them anymore for whatever reason."

Avril was a bit confused, but decided to accept this as the answer.

"If you two are done exchanging glances and pleasantries, I'd like to get this finished before summer break and before you go on wandering in the night."

"Heh, I know that one, I sang it at the Pitch Perfect Pub once", said Avril as they went in.

Headmaster Turner was indeed in a meeting and was astonished to see the trio storming his office.

"Hello there. Didn't my assistant tell you I was in a meeting? It's a very important one that I can't be disturbed from", he said, excusing himself for a few minutes to the person he was talking to.

Adrian started analyzing the headmaster's body language and appearance for a bit to see if he was lying or not. He noticed a bit of fidgeting, some hand gestures after he was done speaking, and avoiding eye contact for some reason. He then turned towards Avril and asked her in a whispered voice:

"What's your verdict, lying or not?"

"Definitely lying, his composure is way different than when I was were not so long ago."

Having a second confirmed lying diagnostic, he answered in a confident tone:

"No, sir, I don't believe you are in such an important meeting. Your lovely assistant made very little effort to stop us coming in. And with you now also rolling your lips, I can only assume you're on some slightly embarrassing online meeting. It's either a loved one, which is negated by the fact that it's actually not important, or with someone from another high school, which given your slightly increased fidgeting, seems to be the case."

Realizing he had been caught, the headmaster took no defensive actions when Adrian attempted to look into his computer screen, where he noticed a slightly bored Jessica Larson. Reminiscing about Steven's antics from

172

when they chose the artists, he took the microphone and asked in an incredibly exaggerated accent:

"Oi, hello there dear old Jess, have you found musical greatness yet?"

Avril and Steven were barely containing their laughter, professor Larson was fuming, while headmaster Turner scrambled to end the call, saying they'll have to circle back later.

"Circle back? What does that even mean, do you attach some tails and run around in circles trying to catch them, like a dog?" asked Adrian.

"Mr. Milner, you have about five seconds to give me one good reason not to send the three of you to detention right now."

"One good reason? I have about six of them right here", answered Adrian, taking out a second copy of all six complaints against Ryan.

Obviously expecting something easily to debunk, the headmaster took the papers with an air of smug confidence, but that gradually changed as he went through each of them, and realized what had been going on for basically the whole school year.

"These are very valid complaints, Mr. Milner."

"Good start, since you're not claiming they're fake. Now, I ask you, headmaster Turner, for one good reason why no action was taken and he was so close to taking out my headphones out of frustration because I called him out on his attitude", said Adrian, his voice and tone much more polite.

Professor Turner looked at Adrian in shock. He knew the story about the last time such a thing happened from professor Stevens, who heard it from Adrian. The story was also confirmed by Steven, who was present at the incident.

"Well, Mr. Milner, I shall now give you six reasons why no actions were taken. This is the first time I have laid eyes on these complaints. I didn't call them fake because I recognized the format, and also because I know your grades and evolution as a songwriter. I made an educated guess that you simply couldn't have enough time for learning how to create such a good forgery. Also, professors generally see you as an honest student."

"What do you mean you didn't see them? Don't you get notified or something when such a complaint is posted?"

"I did get notified in the past, though I had requested for that feature to be disabled since it resulted in too many e-mails for me to delete. What I have been doing instead is checking the portal every morning when I arrive at my office. I have not seen these complaints appear there before."

It was Adrian's turn to be confused. What could possibly have happened? Was the headmaster lying again? Adrian tried to check for any signs of that, but couldn't find any.

"May I see the complaints page myself, just to see how it shows up? Ms. Lawson here tells me you're not a fan of modern technology", said Adrian, adding a bit of an exaggeration to Avril's last name, while looking at her. She thought about pointing to one of the fingers on her left hand, but decided against it, as she didn't want to incur a reprimand for rude gestures.

John Turner loaded up the page and the first thing Adrian noticed was an error popup. He didn't get the message at first, but when he refreshed the page, he noticed that the message said something like "*Missing parent information for 6 child rows.*"

"*Programmer speak is so exhausting...*" he thought to himself. However, the key piece of information was the number of child rows that were missing information.

"Well, I found your culprit, it seems convenient that it's missing information for exactly the number of complaints that I have."

"Yes, these errors have been appearing for quite some time. I tried contacting the people who created the portal for a few weeks now, but they're always swamped, or so they say."

Adrian stopped to think for a few seconds, and then proposed the following:

"I may have a solution to this issue, although it's not exactly what you would call ethical. In that regard, neither is allowing this to fester for as long as you did because you didn't think to investigate further, but that seems to be a recurring theme of your time as headmaster."

Professor Turner gave Adrian a very cold stare, but deep down he knew he was right. There were times such as these when he let things slide too much out of control, which is why he reluctantly agreed to listen to the proposal.

Adrian's solution involved calling Parker, who had enough computer knowledge to be able to hack into the local database of the high school portal and who indeed found that each and every time a new complaint was created, it also saved entries in a different place so as to have a history and timeline on the different statuses that the complaint went through.

Realizing that there was indeed some foul play, the headmaster agreed to overlook Adrian's brash behavior and Parker's unethical but revealing hacking. Parker also deleted the extra information for Adrian's complaints, so the error message no longer appeared, and John Turner could now also inform the tech company that their issues had been solved.

"So, what was the all-important meeting about?" asked Adrian as professor Turner ended the phone call with the tech company.

"Headmaster Larson called to gloat about her high school winning the competition again. I have little faith in next year's bands as well, so I guess I have to look forward to more misery. I was always hoping to lead Gordon High to at least one more victory as headmaster..."

John Turner's voice seemed to trail off at the end there. Did he have so little faith in Adrian and Steven's band attempt, or was there yet another mystery regarding this whole ordeal?

The headmaster soon regained a bit of composure and sent the four students on their way. Parker and the trio said goodbye to each other and started walking home. The trio was happy that Adrian's issues with Ryan were solved, at least for now, but their meeting with the headmaster left them with even more questions.

Parker had confirmed that Ryan's computer skills were not nearly advanced enough to pull such a thing, which was believable since Ryan was surprised that Adrian had actually put in complaints against him.

"We definitely need to dig further", said Avril.

"Yeah. I just hope we're not digging just to wake up in an early grave or graveyard rather, filled with no useful information", added Adrian.

Something foul was happening and they had no idea who was behind it. It looks like summer break was coming just in time.

Summer holiday plans

"Do you think it's possible that Turner himself deleted those things and then acted dumb?" asked Steven.

"I am not entirely sure it's acting..." noted Avril.

"He wasn't acting, and you know it as well as I do", a contemplative but bemused Adrian added. "Why do I have a feeling it's in some way connected to the expelled students from the last 30 years?"

As they were getting ready to head on home, Avril said to Adrian:

"I didn't get a chance to say it earlier, but nice counters on Ryan's attempt to take your headphones off."

"Thanks. As I mentioned, Dad is friends with a sensei so I stopped right there and said that I wanted to learn some defensive maneuvers for moments like this. I kept my eyes open to see if either you or Steven would react in any way to Ryan's probable stupidity. When I saw you pointing, I knew what was coming and could counter it."

Before leaving the building, Adrian said:

"Go on alone for a bit, I need to use the restroom first."

After he was done, they started walking home. Avril then asked:

"So, what's the plan now? Do we try and find out more about this mystery ourselves?"

"Yes, 'cause I won't follow up with headmaster Turner unless I have some concrete evidence. He seems rattled by this and I don't know if it's because he's involved or because he was shocked that someone is doing something behind his back."

When they reached their usual parting point, they said goodbye to each other and went home.

The final three weeks of the school year went by without any noticeable events. Ryan managed to come to a compromise regarding his antics, which involved him staying in detention after school two hours each day as punishment for his behavior.

He wasn't happy with this, but the alternative was to come in during summer break, which was not something he wanted to do either. Ryan's parents were absolutely livid with his conduct, while he was working meticulously on some form of revenge against Adrian.

As the final day of school arrived, the sun was shining brightly as Adrian, Steven and the rest of the band were discussing holiday plans. Having five songs finished was Adrian's goal at the beginning of their adventure as a band and he was overjoyed at having met it, even though it was really tough at times. The band agreed that during the summer, they shall keep practicing the finished songs, while also working on some new ones should any ideas pop up.

The high school rehearsal room was to remain open during summer break for those who wanted to come in and practice, based on the same schedule used during the school year, with the added mention that some extra spots had now become available since this year's competition was now over.

With all of this settled, Adrian and Steven were once again joined by Avril as they started walking home:

"So, what plans do the terrific nerdy twins have for summer holiday?"

"Well, you know, the classics. A seaside holiday, maybe some trips to Cantasia, depending on time and money. Steven also said he wants to go and do some acting classes and he also wants to hit the gym for a bit, with the official excuse being he wants to look and act more like a lead singer. What about you, are you going to go looking for your happy ending?" asked Adrian.

"If only. Pops wants us to have some bonding time and he filled almost all three months with some trips, either at the seaside or through the countryside. It sounds nice on paper but I was hoping for more some down time as well", replied Avril, looking longingly either in the distance or towards Steven, who himself asked:

"So, when exactly are you going town?"

"The last week of summer break if I remember correctly."

"Oh, that's when we're supposed to be in Cantasia, I think. Maybe we can catch up during the last weekend before school starts."

"Yeah, I think I'd love that", she answered, with a subtle smile.

It was Adrian's turn to look heavenward, wondering when these two will finally figure out what's going on. As they arrived at the usual place they split up, he said:

"I'm going to give you two a few minutes alone, if you don't mind." The two nodded in agreement and Adrian gave them some space.

Adrian then thought to himself:

"You know, I always thought I was giving up my principles when accepting this one as our friend. But it feels like this isn't giving up per se. No, this is letting go of things that don't serve me and learning to accept others more easily. I just hope it's worth it. Bah, who am I kidding, it is worth it..."

Steven and Avril then started talking to each other:

"You know, we spent so much time together these last few months it's going to feel like a weird time now. I don't really want to go that long without seeing you", said Steven, blushing for a bit.

"Well, we have phones, we could use those fancy apps that allow us to do video calls if you want. We'll figure out some times via text", a slightly blushing Avril replied.

"Yeah, I'd very much be down with that."

"Sounds like a plan then."

The two of them spent the next few seconds fidgeting a bit, not knowing exactly what they should do.

Steven then looked towards his brother, who seemed to be staring at the sun, and said, while turning back towards Avril:

"Well, I really should be going, it's been a while since Adrian last glitched and I want to see how long he can keep it go - sudden hug!" He was interrupted by Avril once again hugging him very strongly.

"*You know what, I stand by what I said some time ago, hugs really are nice*", he thought to himself, as the weird feeling in his stomach once again returned, possibly even stronger this time.

As the three of them said goodbye to each other and went off home, they were all ready to embrace the freedom of the next three months. Adrian knew that he had to dig deep to try and find any sort of information regarding the two, possibly three mysteries that have unfolded in the last few months.

However, he was more than happy to have this as a pastime. And though he would never admit it out loud, he too was going to miss being around Avril for the next three months. He found that having someone like her to bounce ideas around helped him figure out things faster. And more importantly, she truly was a good friend to him.

"How are you finding things so far? You know, regarding high school, the competition, and so on." asked Steven.

"Well, it's been a case of '*out with the old dreams I've borrowed about the meaning of this thing*'. People put too much emphasis on this competition and lose the fun in making music. So yeah, the path I'll call from here on out will be me own regarding it, and if the path will be my own, it will probably make it easier."

After a short break, Adrian continued:

"As for high school, it's been better than I imagined, but I could still do without some annoyances caused by people like Ryan. Can't have them all, I guess. At least I have the mysteries to spend time on in between songwriting and practice and whatnot."

"I get that. I, for one, am looking forward to the summer. I might actually have fun at those acting classes, might learn a thing or two that may become useful in the long run."

It was a beautiful day, so after they got home, the boys ate lunch and decided to go and play outside, fully embracing the free time ahead of them.

The songs so far

Hello dear reader, Adrian Milner here. Phew, those were some interesting times...or terribly boring, depending on your favorite genre, but I don't hold grudges, and neither does Millie.

Now, listening to the actual songs we worked on would be quite impossible since this is in fact a book. However, I managed to establish a successful connection to the outside world through Millie and you can actually listen to them in an older form.

Millie did say something about working on a revamped version of them, which will be released, according to him, at...some point in time.

Make sure to follow him on Spotify and listen to them in their current version. You can find his profile by searching for Andrew Milner and the songs we have ready so far are called:

1. The Rush (to be revamped)

2. Graduation (to be revamped)

3. Yearn

4. Angry With Yourself

5. Accept Yourself (might be revamped)

With that said, I'm going to go enjoy my summer break now. See you in the next book and wish me luck in finding new song ideas and trying to figure out what sort of tomfoolery is going on at our high school.

.

www.ingramcontent.com/pod-product-compliance
Lightning Source LLC
Chambersburg PA
CBHW070704280626
47159CB00022B/1941